The Executioner burst into the back room and immediately crouched

The instinctual move saved Bolan's life as the escapee burst from behind a desk and triggered two rounds that whizzed overhead close enough for him to hear their passage. He recognized the shooter instantly.

Bolan leveled his weapon and squeezed the trigger. The 9 mm slugs struck center mass, entering the body with an upward trajectory, and punched through lung and heart tissue before exiting out the upper back. The impact sent the man reeling into a filing cabinet with enough force to dent the thin, light gray metal drawers.

The sounds of battle died and Bolan rose slowly amid the smoke of gunfire and the smell of death. The air of violence and spent energies clung to the Executioner like a cloak. The battle had taken less than a minute but the threat had been quelled.

All that remained was to topple the head of the underworld. And it was a task Mack Bolan relished.

MACK BOLAN ®

The Executioner

The Executioner

Don Pendleton's

HOSTILE ODDS

A GOLD EAGLE BOOK FROM

WORLDWIDE®

TORONTO • NEW YORK • LONDON
AMSTERDAM • PARIS • SYDNEY • HAMBURG
STOCKHOLM • ATHENS • TOKYO • MILAN
MADRID • WARSAW • BUDAPEST • AUCKLAND

Recycling programs
for this product may
not exist in your area.

First edition March 2009

ISBN-13: 978-0-373-64364-6
ISBN-10:   0-373-64364-0

Special thanks and acknowledgment to
Jon Guenther for his contribution to this work.

HOSTILE ODDS

War grows out of the desire of the individual to gain advantage at the expense of his fellow man.

—Napoleon Hill
1883–1970

My war grew out of opposing those who oppress the weak and exploit the innocent. In that respect, it is a war the enemy has declared on itself.

—Mack Bolan

THE
MACK BOLAN
LEGEND

Nothing less than a war could have fashioned the destiny of the man called Mack Bolan. Bolan earned the Executioner title in the jungle hell of Vietnam.

But this soldier also wore another name—Sergeant Mercy. He was so tagged because of the compassion he showed to wounded comrades-in-arms and Vietnamese civilians.

Mack Bolan's second tour of duty ended prematurely when he was given emergency leave to return home and bury his family, victims of the Mob. Then he declared a one-man war against the Mafia.

He confronted the Families head-on from coast to coast, and soon a hope of victory began to appear. But Bolan had broken society's every rule. That same society started gunning for this elusive warrior—to no avail.

So Bolan was offered amnesty to work within the system against terrorism. This time, as an employee of Uncle Sam, Bolan became Colonel John Phoenix. With a command center at Stony Man Farm in Virginia, he and his new allies—Able Team and Phoenix Force—waged relentless war on a new adversary: the KGB.

But when his one true love, April Rose, died at the hands of the Soviet terror machine, Bolan severed all ties with Establishment authority.

Now, after a lengthy lone-wolf struggle and much soul-searching, the Executioner has agreed to enter an "arm's-length" alliance with his government once more, reserving the right to pursue personal missions in his Everlasting War.

Prologue

Klamath Falls, Oregon

The two F-15E Eagle fighter jets streaked into the air with the thunderclap of sonic speed, their aluminum skins glinting silvery-blue with the twilight of dusk. Suddenly they lost altitude and crashed several hundred yards outside the perimeter fence of Kingsley Airfield.

The tower crew could only discern what looked like engine flameouts, and then the explosions of impact a heartbeat later, each red-orange fireball fed by twenty thousand liters of jet fuel. As one controller began to scream out the call signs of the two trainer fighters, the tower chief contacted the command duty officer at the USAF headquarters building. The CDO ordered an immediate lockdown of the base and surrounding area even as the tower dispatched emergency services to the crash site.

The tower crew would later testify they hadn't seen anything out of the ordinary, even swore the flashes of light just prior to the accident could only have been reflections of the engine flame-outs. What they didn't know—couldn't possibly have known at that time and what the government wouldn't tell them—were that those flashes marked the points where surface-to-air rockets had struck the pair of trainer fighters.

Rockets fired from portable launchers in proximity to the airfield.

"Which meant is wasn't an accident at all," the chief investigator told the CDO and Colonel Harlan Winnetka, the wing commander, a week later.

"Any ideas who the hell might be responsible for these attacks?" Winnetka asked.

"I can't be certain of anything right now, sir," the investigator replied. "To be perfectly honest, there isn't enough evidence to draw a definitive conclusion. The only thing we know for sure is that these craft were brought down by shoulder-fired weapons. The perpetrators were diligent to cover their tracks in the confusion, because we were too busy working this initially as an accident, maybe a midair collision. After all, these were trainers with students at the stick. We thought one of the students lost control and ran into the other, bringing down both birds in the process."

"Except that those fighters were also attended by highly experienced pilots," Winnetka said. "And with the evidence of anti-aircraft weapons, we know different. Could this be the work of terrorists?"

Major Leonard Swope, the CDO on duty at the time of the incident, expressed incredulity. "You think these were…terrorists? If that gets out to the press, sir—"

"Well, then we just make damned sure it *doesn't* get out, Major!" Winnetka's face reddened. He jabbed a finger at the investigator and his eyes flashed. "And I don't even have the details of this incident off to Washington yet, so you have to promise you'll keep quiet about this until I can make a full report to the Chief of Staff. Is that understood, Captain?"

The investigator nodded. "Yes, sir, of course. But I must submit my written report within forty-eight hours."

"I'm aware of the regulations, mister," Winnetka said. "I have no desire to make this sound like a cover-up. I just don't want a media circus. If either of you are approached by *anyone* about this, you simply advise them it's still under investigation. In fact, better to just refer them to me."

After he swore both officers to secrecy and warned of the consequences should they disobey his direct orders, Winnetka dismissed them. He spun in his leather office chair and looked absently out the window.

Winnetka had put out feelers and gotten just the response he expected—the shock of suggesting a terrorist group might be responsible for another attack on American soil had practically sent his two subordinates into a fit. What they didn't know, either because they were too blind or too afraid to admit it, was that domestic terrorist activities across the Northwest had increased in recent months. Winnetka didn't know exactly who or what, but he couldn't ignore the signs. The Pentagon would call him paranoid, maybe even suggest he take some leave to reconsider his assertions without hard evidence, but at least he could prove this had been a wanton attack against the United States Air Force and not just a training accident. Either way, he needed help on this—a specialized kind of help.

And he had no idea where to find it.

1

Mack Bolan stared at a face of death through the crosshairs of a Bushnell 6 x 42 electronic scope.

He tightened the ergonomic stock of the SIG-Sauer SSG-300 against his shoulder and took a deep breath. The Swiss had designed the rifle to provide high accuracy stats, increasing the one-shot kill probability by a factor of ten, and the 7.62 mm NATO rounds averaged a muzzle velocity of eight hundred meters per second. The rifle would do the job nicely in Bolan's hands.

Organized crime had brought the Executioner to the sleepy town of Tulelake in northern California. In fact, the Gowan crime Family had taken over all the vice action throughout Siskiyou County, from prostitution and drugs to a comprehensive numbers racket. The Executioner had spent the past month in meticulous soft probes of the communities throughout the county, and one thing remained consistent: Mickey Gowan's fingers were into a very large pie. Mack Bolan had a plan to chop them to nubs.

He would start with Gowan's right-hand man, Billy Moran.

Bolan would have preferred to do this at some other place and time, but he'd seen an opportunity to bring down one of the big players in the Gowan crime Family without endangering bystanders. Moran and Gowan were almost never seen together other than behind the ten-foot-high walls of Gowan's estate, additionally fortified by several dozen well-armed house soldiers. Bolan hadn't let that dissuade him, however, since Moran was like most human beings—a creature of habit and therefore predictable. The Executioner decided to exploit that vulnerability to send a message loud and clear.

He let out half his deep breath and squeezed the trigger. The big rifle boomed a thunderous report, but Bolan kept it rock steady against his shoulder until he verified the kill. Shock flashed across Moran's face at the same moment his head snapped sideways at an odd angle. Blood and fragments of skull erupted from the wound, spraying the lieutenant who sat next to him, and then he disappeared behind the table at which he'd been sitting as the impact knocked him completely out of his seat.

Bolan played the bolt smoothly and chambered a fresh round before the three bodyguards at Moran's private table on the back patio of the Irish café could react. Moran's lieutenant went next. The Executioner caught him with a clean shot to the center of the chest. The shot knocked him off his feet, and he crashed through the lead glass top of a neighboring table.

Bringing another round home, Bolan sighted carefully on the third man, now concealed behind the thick ivy intertwined through the wrought-iron fencing that bordered the porch. Apparently, the goon figured the shooter couldn't see him if he couldn't see the shooter. He was wrong. Bolan took the guy with a shot center mass. The only sign of the hit was a geyser of blood that erupted over the top of the decorative fencing.

Bolan policed his brass, then broke from his position at a wood line about one hundred and fifty yards from the restaurant. He'd specifically selected the spot not only for its distance but also because it would take someone time to reach the area remotely, and even longer for them to actually figure out from exactly where Bolan had fired the shots. By that time, the Executioner would be long gone.

Bolan reached his rental car parked two hundred yards from the woods on a dirt access road. He buried the rifle in a predug pit just off the shoulder and covered it with natural leaves. He marked a tree near the brush with reactive chalk that would glow when sprayed with a reagent and then hightailed it out of there.

If he did get pulled over by the local authorities, he certainly wouldn't want them to find him with any weapons.

As he left the dirt road and entered the city limits of Tulelake, he considered his next move. Word had it that Gowan used the numbers rackets to help launder money for parties unknown, a lot of which took place in underground gambling joints scattered throughout Siskiyou County. Bolan couldn't help but wonder how those parties might feel if a whole bunch of the cash running through those joints suddenly came up missing. The warrior figured he'd find out soon enough.

The Executioner just happened to have an address.

THE BROWN-AND-GRAY HAZE of cigar and cigarette smoke clung in low clouds throughout the dimly lit room. A jazz-funk mix blared from unseen speakers in the background, competing with the steady din of voices, laughter and shouts of excitement. People were scattered around gaming tables of different venues, and with the décor, wall-length bar, cigarette and drink gals in miniskirts to complete the ensemble, Bolan got the impression he'd entered a 1930s speakeasy.

After returning to his lodgings for a shower and change of clothes, Bolan drove to the popular joint just outside Tulelake on Highway 139. The Executioner paid his cover of five hundred in cash to a pair of gorillas watching the basement entrance and allowed them to pat him down. He felt naked without his constant companion, the Beretta 93-R, but drawing attention before the right time was the last thing he wanted to do. Better to play the game and wait it out, see what happened. Bolan mingled, played a couple hands of blackjack, cashed out when he reached two hundred dollars, and then lost the entire winnings along with an additional half bill at the only roulette table in the place. He played the other tables for the next two hours, keeping one eye on the game and the other on the room's occupants, focusing on individual conversations.

The sounds of a mild disturbance at the front entrance caught his attention, and he let his eyes rove in that direction while maintaining a discreet posture. He saw the two thugs hassle a shorter man with a dark suit and a haircut that spelled Fed. The newcomer had the smell of cop all over him, and while the hoods at the door might have suspected it, Bolan knew it for a fact because he'd met him early the previous morning.

Bolan lost his final hand of the evening, dropped his remaining three chips on the dealer as a tip and moved toward the door at a casual pace. As he went to slide past the cop still trying to get in the door, the warrior slammed hard into the smaller man and nearly knocked him off his feet. The guy turned toward Bolan in irritation and opened his mouth, but the view shocked him into silence.

The Executioner took his mind off it before the idiot got them both killed. "Sorry, Tiny, didn't see you there." He flashed the door guards a semiwicked grin and then walked out.

The man continued arguing with the bouncers for another minute, probably just to make it look good, then joined Bolan outside the restaurant that sat directly above the underground club.

"Why do I feel the compunction to punch your lights out?" Special Agent Jeff Kellogg demanded.

"Lack of common sense," Bolan said as he turned and headed for his car.

"Wait a minute, Cooper!" Kellogg called, using Bolan's cover name for the mission. The Fed trotted to get ahead of Bolan's long strides. He stopped in the Executioner's path and held up a hand, careful not to touch the imposing form. "I don't know where you're from or who you work for, but I thought I made it clear yesterday to butt out."

"I don't take orders from you, Kellogg," Bolan said flatly. "And don't blame me because you couldn't get in. You got any idea where you were just now?"

Kellogg tried to look confident but seemed to falter under Bolan's scrutiny.

"I didn't think so," Bolan continued. "In case it escaped notice, you were facing off with Mickey Gowan's boys."

"What? That's impossible!"

"And it's exactly that kind of thinking that'll get you killed one of these days," Bolan said. "Count me out."

"What proof you got Gowan's running that operation?"

"Plenty. I tried to bring it to you nearly three weeks ago, and you didn't seem interested."

"I'm interested now. But I'm not a law unto myself, pal, and I damned sure can't just go busting down doors without hard evidence. The only things you brought me were theories and conjecture. The FBI doesn't operate speculatively."

"Maybe you should start," Bolan said as he walked around Kellogg and continued toward his car.

"You're not bulletproof, Cooper!" Kellogg called after Bolan. "Don't go doing something stupid, or I'll bust you in no time flat."

The soldier got into his car and split. Kellogg was too obtuse to realize Bolan had probably just saved his hide. Bolan considered his options as he drove back to his room at the Tulelake lodge. He'd just left one of many of Mickey Gowan's operations. But while some of the people at that underground casino were helping to line Gowan's pockets, Bolan couldn't categorize them in the same class as the crime boss. Many were there simply to have some fun, and certainly hadn't done anything worthy of the Executioner's wrath. Besides, Bolan had what he needed. Something big was happening just over the border in Timber Vale, one of the lumber towns north of Klamath Falls. Less than a two-hour drive from Tulelake, it was filled with lumberjacks, mill workers and carpenters. The mill there also had a union, which was run by one of Gowan's underlings.

As Bolan drew closer to the lakeside lodge where he'd been staying, he noticed two pairs of headlights swing into the review mirror. The hairs on the back of his neck stood on end. He'd driven this road enough to know it was practically devoid of traffic this time of night. Despite the fact this was tourist season in Siskiyou County, he could chalk up a single vehicle to coincidence but not two.

Bolan increased speed as soon as he rounded a curve and the lights disappeared, then he pumped the brakes and swung the wheel hard left. Halfway into the turn he released the brake and floored the accelerator, jerking the wheel back to the right and then hard left again. Bolan maneuvered out of the power slide and stopped cold, his car now pointed the way he'd come. He kept one hand on the wheel while he reached over to the glove compartment, popped the latch and withdrew the Beretta 93-R. He placed it on the seat next to him and waited.

A few seconds elapsed before the first tail car rounded the bend and its occupants found Bolan's rental directly in their path. Bolan caught the flash of surprise in the driver's face as he cranked the wheel and slammed on the brakes to avoid a head-on collision. The Executioner dropped into low gear, depressed the brake and spun his wheels by putting pedal to metal in hopes his opposition would think he was trying to flee. The tactic worked and the tail car immediately swung around to pursue—right into the path of their backup car just now rounding the curve.

The second vehicle T-boned the first, and then Bolan released the brake and floored the accelerator. He put a little distance between the two vehicles and then pulled to the shoulder and backed into a private road leading into the darkness of the woods. When he'd proceeded about fifty yards he killed his lights and engine. Bolan reached beneath his sport coat and withdrew his cellular phone. He would have preferred to use a pay phone, given it had better security than wireless, but such weren't always the luxuries of field operations.

The voice of Johnny Gray answered on the second ring. "What do you say, Sarge?"

Only two men had ever called him that: Jack Grimaldi, ace pilot for Stony Man, and Johnny Gray, Bolan's brother.

"Hey," Bolan replied. "We're not secure."

"Got you," Johnny said.

"I need you to look into something for me," Bolan continued.

"Start gathering intelligence on a place called Timber Vale. It's a logging town just north of Klamath Falls, Oregon."

"What are you looking for?"

"Not sure yet…just anything unusual or different."

"You thinking of heading that way?"

"It crossed my mind. Can you find out and get back to me?"

Johnny paused for a moment, and Bolan could hear the faint clack of a computer keyboard. A moment later, Johnny said, "Give me an hour."

"You got it."

As Bolan hung up the phone, he saw one of the pursuit vehicles race past the road. He smiled, placed the phone on the seat next to the Beretta and started the engine. He turned onto the road that would take him down the hill and eventually lead to Highway 139. He could leave his belongings at the lodge for now—he was paid up through the month. Something told Bolan the answers he sought awaited him in Oregon.

In a town called Timber Vale.

JOHNNY GOT BACK to his brother with the information in the time frame he promised.

"There have indeed been some eye-opening activities," he told the Executioner.

"Like what?" Bolan asked.

"I hooked up a secure-shell Telnet to Bear's system at Stony Man," Johnny said. "About a week ago, two F-15E training fighters crashed as they took off from Kingsley Airfield. You familiar with that area?"

"Slightly," Bolan said, searching his almost eidetic memory. "It's an Oregon Air National Guard base."

"Right. Preliminary information has already been fed through the Pentagon's computer systems, which of course was no trouble for Bear to access."

Bolan believed it. Aaron "The Bear" Kurtzman, cybernetics wizard and leader of Stony Man Farm's in-house technology team, had saved countless lives with his uncanny ability to deliver the right intelligence at the right time.

"Who's in charge there?"

"A guy by the name of Colonel Harlan Winnetka."

The name didn't ring any bells, but Bolan filed it away. "What else you have?"

"Well, like I said, the official reports aren't in but we *think* the jets were shot down, possibly by the Earth Liberation Front."

The FBI had first classified the ELF a domestic terrorist organization in 2001. Membership in the ELF had sprung from the Earth First movement that originated in Brighton, England. Catching the ELF's highest ranking members had proved more than difficult for the FBI and other agencies. Its rolls were highly secretive, its meetings held in diverse places and infrequently, and it almost never claimed action for acts that were clearly driven by concerns with ecology and ecosystems.

"That's interesting but I don't see how it ties to what I'm looking at," Bolan replied.

"I would have agreed until I started digging deeper into the ELF's history," Johnny said. "For a lot of years their activities declined in the Northwestern states, particularly in Washington, Montana, Oregon and Utah. They sort of went silent in that area along with two other major domestic terrorist groups."

"Who?"

"You might not believe it when I tell you."

The Executioner chuckled. "Try me."

"The Aryan Brotherhood and the Militia for Liberation from Government."

Bolan took note as he passed the sign welcoming him to Oregon, and then said, "Probably both of which shared membership."

"Right," Johnny said. "And that means they also would have shared financing."

"Sure. It's no secret these types of groups dip into joint coffers. Pooling their fiscal resources makes them stronger."

"Yes, but it's interesting that only ELF-related activities are on the rise there again," Johnny said. "Not those two groups or any others, for that matter."

"Which means they're now getting their money from someone else," Bolan concluded.

"It's a good bet, Mack."

"Nice work," Bolan replied. "And you're right, it's definitely interesting."

"Mind if I ask a question?"

"Shoot," Bolan said.

"Do you really think there's a connection between Gowan's activities and this latest incident? I mean, we don't have any proof the ELF is actually behind this attack on the Oregon Air National Guard."

"I'm not sure yet how it would benefit Gowan to fund the ELF, particularly when a lot of his work would seem at cross-purposes. But I know Gowan's dug in deep in Timber Vale, and as that happens to be right near Klamath Falls and it's a large source of revenue for the entire area, I have to think it's worth checking out."

"Fair enough," Johnny replied. "I trust your instincts."

"Let's just hope I'm right," the Executioner said. "I'll be in touch."

"Live large, bro."

2

FBI Special Agent Jefferson Kellogg mentally rehearsed his announcement for a sixth time as he negotiated the winding drive that led to Mickey Gowan's estate. Kellogg had warned Billy Moran to keep a low profile, and as usual the cocky Irish bastard hadn't listened to him. Now he was dead, and Kellogg had the terrible task of breaking the news personally to Gowan.

Kellogg had no doubts about who was probably behind the hit: Matt Cooper. That guy had a habit of turning up where he was least welcome, and his nosiness didn't set well with Kellogg. He had it under control, and he didn't need some outsider meddling in his affairs. The fact Kellogg refused to admit he didn't really have any control over the situation had nothing to do with it.

Kellogg parked his car, exited and tossed the keys to Gowan's wheelman, who doubled as valet when he wasn't chauffeuring the old man around.

"Take care of her, will you, Sid?"

The young man, who was barely twenty if he was a day, almost didn't catch the keys but he managed to one-hand them at the last moment. Kellogg pretended not to see the dirty look Sid Harper fired his way, and a smile played across his lips as he sauntered up the flagstone steps and stabbed the doorbell. A melodious chime echoed from somewhere within and the door opened a moment later to reveal one of Gowan's house soldiers. The guy looked unfamiliar to Kellogg.

"Yeah?" he rumbled.

Kellogg stepped inside and looked the man square in the eyes. "I don't recognize you. New here?"

"Started last week," he said. "Who the fuck are you?"

"I'll take care of this, Charlie Boy," a gravelly voice interjected.

Both men turned to see Gowan's personal assistant, Struthers Sullivan, dance down the wide steps at the other end of the reception foyer. "Sully" bore the full Hiberno-English accent and touted himself a pureblood Irishman because he hailed from Dublin, a fact that had elevated him to his current status in the Gowan crime Family. Mickey Gowan had always tried to remain purist when it came to those in his immediate company. He had no problem hiring a Scot or other loose kinsmen, even Irish-Americans, for the "scut" work, but he made damned sure his closest advisers were as close to Irish as Irish could be.

"Well, Sully!" Kellogg said as Charlie Boy closed the heavy front door and then disappeared. "I wouldn't have expected to find you here. I thought Mr. Gowan sent you on a long trip."

"He did," Sully said with a good-natured wink. "Job turned out easier than I expected so I got back early."

Kellogg nodded, well aware of Sully's specialty. When Gowan needed a problem taken care of permanently, he sent Struthers Sullivan. Kellogg always liked Sully, even admired him on some levels, although he didn't trust him at all. Then again, he didn't trust any of them—he knew what they did for a living. He'd spent his entire career putting away men like Sully until he discovered exactly how much money he could make playing for the other team. When he agreed to come over and work for Gowan, he insisted on only two things: he'd answer only to the old man, and any remuneration had to be unmarked and untraceable cash. For a guy like Mickey Gowan, neither request seemed out of line. And fifteen hundred a week to get a federal cop at Kellogg's level in his pocket was chump change.

"Where's the old man?" Kellogg asked.

"Upstairs with the missus," Sully replied.

Kellogg knew what that meant. Mickey Gowan actually had

three or four in his little harem, all of whom lived in different states and traveled regularly. The one here was actually his legal wife and the others simply mistresses. As Gowan had once told Kellogg, "Running an enterprise like mine leaves a guy with needs no one woman could possibly satisfy."

"Well, I don't want to crash his party," Kellogg said in an all-business tone, "but I got to talk to him right away, Sully. It's important."

Sully jerked his head in the direction of the stairs. "Come on, I'll take you up. They ain't doing nothing special."

Kellogg followed Sully to the second floor, which was as spacious and fancifully decorated as the first, and found Mickey Gowan in the entertainment room, where Gowan spent most of his time with friends and associates. The space took up the entire east wing of Gowan's mansion, and sported the most impressive display of electronics money could buy. A custom-built HDTV with its seventy-two-inch screen and sixteen-channel surround-sound theater system took up nearly one wall. Theater-style seating branched off the central viewing area. Just beyond the seats the low-rise steps spread onto a wall-to-wall raised floor with a full wet bar and a burnished oval table that could easily seat twenty people. Massive mahogany pillars carved with intricate designs sprung up throughout the room. Contrasting honey-oak shelves ran along the exterior walls and supported wood carvings and hand-beaten metal pieces. The term *rustic* came to Kellogg's mind the first time he saw this room.

A fire crackled in a free-standing brick fireplace in the middle of the room, although it had to be at least sixty degrees outside with plenty of humidity. The rumor mill had it that Gowan suffered from some malady that caused him to be cold most of the time, so the guy always kept his place like an oven. Kellogg usually needed a shower after staying in the house any length of time, although he hadn't attributed it to the psychological component of washing away the filth that surrounded him.

Music played quietly over the hardwired entertainment system.

It sounded to Kellogg like something from the *River Dance,* but he ignored the Gaelic-style tune. He'd heard enough of that shit to last him a lifetime. Gowan was hunched over a pool table, his bushy white eyebrows furrowed in concentration. His wife, Glenda, sat on a padded leather barstool while she nursed a sweating beer. Although nearly fifty, Gowan's wife had the figure of a twenty-year-old, and Kellogg had to force himself to avert his eyes from the shapely legs in fishnet stockings that dangled seductively from the denim miniskirt.

Kellogg started forward and opened his mouth, but Sully put a finger to his lips and blocked the approach with a hand against Kellogg's chest. Kellogg stopped in his tracks and bit his tongue. He folded his arms and waited at a respectful distance until Gowan took his shot. He missed banking the green No. 6 into a corner pocket by a long shot. Gowan cursed as he straightened and only then did he recognize the two arrivals.

Mickey Gowan looked at them a moment before his scowl transformed into a smile as false as that of a crooked televangelist. Kellogg didn't trust Gowan any more than he trusted Sully, and he genuinely liked Sully. Part of it had to do with the fact Gowan treated him more like a hired hand than a partner—not that Kellogg had any high ideals about their relationship. And at least Gowan had been true to his word, which was fine as long as the old man kept the money coming.

"Jefferson, good to see you," Gowan said. He stepped forward and extended a hand.

Kellogg took it with reticence; the old man had a slimy shake. "Sure. You too, Mickey." He hated it when Gowan called him Jefferson. Christ, even his mother hadn't called him that, and she'd named him.

"You want a drink?"

"No, thanks," he said. "Mickey, I have some bad news. I think maybe you're going to want to sit down for it."

"I'm not a fuckin' old man, see? I think I can take whatever you have to tell me, so out with 'er."

"Okay," Kellogg said, surprised at his enjoyment when he blurted, "Billy Moran's dead."

The room was so silent Kellogg wondered for a moment whether Gowan had heard him. Something fell in the old man's countenance. The light went out of his azure-colored eyes, and his face went nearly the same shade of white as the shock of unkempt hair matted across his head.

"Stop the lights!" Sully cut in. "You didn't tell me *that* was the news, ya yonker. Sorry, boss."

After the old man's lip quivered for a time, he finally said through gritted teeth, "Who? Who did this, Jefferson?"

"I don't know yet. But I got my suspicions."

"Who?"

"Like I said, Mickey, I don't know—"

"I don't give a shite! I wanna know who yer suspect!"

Kellogg felt his face flush as he replied, "Cooper…a guy named Matt Cooper."

"Who is he?"

"I don't know. But I think he might work for the U.S. government."

"FBI? One of your guys?"

Kellogg shook his head. "Shit no, Mickey. If it were that simple, I'd already know about him right now. No, he doesn't come up in anything I run his name through."

"Well, what the hell does that mean?" Sully demanded.

"I'm not sure." Kellogg shrugged and continued, "He could be a special operative of some kind, although black ops are technically illegal in the U.S. unless it has to do with terrorism."

Kellogg couldn't swear to it, but he thought he noticed a silent exchange between Sully and Gowan. Gowan was basically a glorified labor bully, with his fingers mostly into the most basic of the vices: illegal gambling, numbers and cons. He was also involved in prostitution and drugs, but Kellogg had learned to overlook that minor indiscretion. Recently, however, Gowan had got himself caught up in dealings with the Earth

Liberation Front, and that little fact had started to make Kellogg nervous. Gowan wasn't aware that Kellogg already knew about his relationship with the ELF. For the sake of plausible deniability and to protect his own interests, Kellogg decided to act as if he didn't.

"If this guy's onto us at all, boss, we need to get rid of him," Sully declared.

Gowan nodded. "Ya, and it don't mean shite to me if we can prove the bastard busted a cap on Billy or not."

"That's where I might be able to help," Kellogg said.

"What do you mean?" Gowan asked.

"If he is operating illegally, then that would be enough for me to open an official investigation inside the Bureau. At best, he could be a freelancer, in which case he's still operating illegally. And if he isn't sanctioned and he did kill Moran then that's homicide. We might be able to bring him in on that alone if I can get enough evidence."

"Who's looking into it right now?" Sully asked.

Kellogg shrugged. "Well, since it happened in Siskiyou County and Tulelake has no real police force to speak of, it will probably fall to the sheriff's office and possibly the state if the locals call for help."

"Naw," Gowan said. "We're already going to have enough cops crawling around here, and I don't need that. Everybody knows Billy Moran was in my employ, and that's going to bring some serious heat on my head."

"Why didn't you know about this guy before?" Sully asked.

"I did," Kellogg admitted with a shrug. "But what the hell do you want me to do? I can't just go rousting someone because he's walking down the sidewalk."

"That's what you get paid for, Kellogg, to keep this kind of shit out of Mickey's hair."

"Never mind that!" Gowan's face got red. "I want this matter cleared up, and I want it done in the next twenty-four. Sully, you're in charge. Kellogg, you follow Sully's instructions and do whatever you can to make sure this Cooper's no longer breathing by Monday, sunrise. You think you can handle that?"

"Yes, Mickey."

"All right, now both of you take a walk. I got some grieving to do." A droplet of a tear had now formed at the corner of Gowan's eye, but neither man dared comment on that. "And Sully, I want you to see to all Billy's arrangements. We'll make sure his old lady gets taken care of."

"Yes, Mickey."

"And his kids," Gowan added. "You got that? We got to make sure we take care of Billy's kids."

"It'll get done, boss."

"And you'll arrange it…personally?"

"Yes, Mickey."

"All right."

THE LUMINOUS HANDS of Mack Bolan's watch read 0130 as he passed the city-limits sign for Timber Vale.

The road dipped down from the north side of the Siskiyou Pass, and a few winding turns brought Bolan to a level approach into Timber Vale. Traffic lights lazily winked red as Bolan slowed enough to take a look around him. He went about three blocks before the glow of a light shimmered through one of the storefront windows. Bolan pulled to the curb and watched for a moment. Three vehicles were parked directly in front of the building, which sported a decorative awning. Bolan eased his rental closer and saw Lamplighter Diner hand scrawled in paint on the glass.

It would be as good a place as any to start.

Bolan left his car and walked up the sidewalk. He checked the vehicles as he passed, verified no occupants and then pushed through the door. A bell tinkled over the squeak of door hinges as Bolan entered. Every eye in the place looked in his direction.

Bolan took an inventory. A middle-aged waitress with ash-blond hair and sun freckles greeted him with half a smile. Two burly men wearing baseball caps, one with a racing logo and the other advertising a well-known trucking firm, looked up from their beers and plates of half-eaten food. A man Bolan marked in his late sixties peered with little interest from around the edge of his newspaper. He wore a flannel coat—a bit crazy considering the heat even that time of the morning—and sported a white Fu Manchu mustache.

"Morning," Bolan greeted them.

The old man went back to his paper, and the two men went back to their food after nodding in his direction. The waitress kept her attention on Bolan with an expression of half wariness, half interest. He walked to the other end of the counter before taking a seat in the booth where he could watch both the large window and the entrance while he kept his back to a solid wall.

"What can I get you?" the waitress asked.

Bolan thought hard a moment about just ordering coffee, but then realized he hadn't eaten since lunch. "Got a menu?"

"Only thing Earl cooks this time of night is the special or fried chicken." She smiled and winked. "We *always* got fried chicken, you know."

"Any good?" Bolan asked.

She looked almost miffed. "Everything Earl makes is good."

"Then in that case…"

Bolan didn't have to finish his sentence. The waitress delivered another half smile, shouted an order to Earl in back and then poured Bolan some coffee unbidden. When she saw the Executioner's questioning gaze, she said sheepishly, "You looked like you could use some joe. Don't worry, it's good, too."

She returned the pot, cleared a few dishes and then said to him, "You new here or just passing through?"

Bolan shrugged. "Depends."

"On what?"

"If I can find some work."

"What do you do?"

"Little bit of everything, I guess," Bolan said. He didn't want to seem too obvious. He could already tell he'd garnered some attention from the two men who, having finished their meals, seemed to hang on every word of his conversation with the waitress. If he came straight out with something directly in their line of business, he might raise suspicions.

"I build houses, mostly," he continued. "Do some electrical or plumbing work here and there."

"Ah," she said. "There's always work to be had for a man who's good with his hands."

While the comment didn't seem offhanded, Bolan could tell the waitress was making a show of flirting with him, particularly in front of the other pair. His eyes snapped quickly to her hand, he saw neither a wedding band nor the remnant of where she'd worn one, so either she was divorced, unmarried or nontraditional. She hadn't made the remark to spark the two men into any type of action; they didn't seem to care one way or another. In fact, it seemed that they had taken more than a passing interest in Bolan. Had he been followed? Were Gowan's men on to him? If so, how had they managed to predict where he'd land?

It seemed too coincidental, but these guys were definitely more than they appeared.

"Do much working with wood?" the man in the trucker cap asked suddenly.

"Like I said, just building houses," Bolan said.

"Never worked in a lumber mill?"

Bolan shook his head. "No, but I'm always willing to learn. Does it pay well?"

"It's honest work," said the man's partner.

The first man withdrew a small card from his pocket and handed it to the waitress to pass to Bolan. "Tell you what, you show up at that address tomorrow morning and ask to talk to the lumber foreman. Louise here can give you directions. Give the foreman that card and tell him I sent you."

"And you are?"

The man got up to leave with his partner and walked over to Bolan. He extended his hand. "Buck…Buck Nordstrom."

Bolan held up the card with a nod. "Thanks."

"No problem," he said. "Grip like that and a guy your size… you'll do a good job, I'm sure."

With that, the two men walked out. It seemed almost too easy to the Executioner, but he decided to play it out and see how things went. Since logging and milling were the major industries in Timber Vale and he knew from casual talks at Tulelake that Mickey Gowan had his hands into everything in the town, all the odds were in his favor. He'd have to play it carefully; there was still a chance, however remote, he was about to walk into a trap.

But for now, the Executioner had his in.

3

With the waitress's help, Mack Bolan managed to find a place to stay for the night. The shabby motel on the edge of town would make a remote and unobtrusive base of operations, but he politely declined Louise's offer to join him. Once settled, Bolan stripped, showered and then crawled between the sheets for a few hours of sleep. The rest did him well, and he was up and moving by dawn.

Bolan dressed in his best working-man duds, a pair of jeans and plaid flannel work shirt with the sleeves rolled to the elbows, and then drove to the address on the card. He didn't know what to expect or even whom to ask for, but that didn't seem to matter; the three large men who met Bolan at the gate had apparently been told to expect him. One man offered to park his car. Bolan agreed without reservation, since he'd elected to pack the Beretta 93-R in a modified shoulder holster that rode high under his left armpit, its bulk concealed by the loose flannel shirt jacket, and nothing remained in the vehicle that would betray his identity. He'd even left some fast-food bags and a few empty beer cans under the seat just to reinforce the cover.

The remaining pair escorted Bolan to a security guard for sign-in and then handed him a hardhat and hearing protection. He declined the muffs with a shake of his head, but one of the men insisted it was policy. Bolan shrugged and donned the equipment. They continued through the mill, and the Executioner used the opportunity to study his surroundings. The earmuffs did a lot to decrease the piercing buzz and whine of saws cutting through massive logs. A few separate areas were crowded with workers running band saws, jigs and even a couple of lathes.

At the other end of the mill, the men escorted Bolan up a flight of metal steps to a second-story landing. They followed a catwalk that eventually terminated at a massive office with a large glass overlooking the mill floor below. An old-fashioned potbelly coal stove stood in one corner. The men showed Bolan to a seat where they indicated he could take off the safety equipment and then made their exit through a side door.

Bolan sat in one of the three chairs positioned beneath the glass window. A young woman with blond hair and blue eyes sat at a computer terminal. He detected a faint clacking sound as the secretary's fingers almost danced over the keyboard. Other than a single furtive glance and a smile she completely ignored him. Bolan considered speaking to her, but the sound of a door opening distracted him. He looked up to see a large man step out. He had red hair, large lips, square jaw and a broad face. He stood at least six-foot-six with meaty forearms and broad shoulders, and he moved powerfully.

His face broke into a grin and he extended a hand as Bolan stood. "How ya be, laddie? Come on in."

Bolan stepped through the doorway into an expansive office that he could only have described as a first-rate pigsty. Books and papers were strewed across a massive desk and equally large tabletop such that no part of their surfaces went untouched. The garbage can overflowed, and the room reeked of cheap whiskey and cigarette smoke. Bolan took a seat as the man wedged himself into a chair about two sizes too small between his desktop and credenza.

"The name's Fagan MacDermott," he began. The Irish accent when he pronounced his name left no doubts in Bolan's mind whom MacDermott worked for. "I understand you're new in town. Maybe lookin' for work?"

Bolan showed him a wan smile. "Word travels fast."

MacDermott shrugged in way of explanation and said, "No more than usual for a small town like this one."

"I noticed you got quite a crew out there. Everybody work for the mill?"

"Hell, pal, the mill's what keeps this town running!" MacDermott burst into laughter.

Bolan considered him uncharacteristically cheerful, but he decided not to push. Not yet. "I'm Matt Cooper. I've been on the road quite a bit, doing some odd jobs here and there."

"On the run from the law?"

"No," Bolan said.

MacDermott fished a cigarette from the pack on his desk, lit it, then sat back in his chair and studied Bolan through a cloud of smoke.

The Executioner remained impassive. He got the impression that if he'd said he was on the run, it probably wouldn't make any difference but he decided not to make it up as he went along. He wasn't working this one for Stony Man and thus he didn't have time to put a real cover in place. If MacDermott decided to look into his criminal history, he figured it was better not to state he had one and then have to explain later why "Matt Cooper" not only had no record, but also had no fingerprints on file.

"It don't make no difference if you got something to hide," MacDermott said. "Best to be honest with me, Coop."

"I've got nothing to hide," Bolan said with a sigh. "And I'm not running from the law. Just looking for maybe a place to settle down. Sleeping and eating out of my car gets a bit old after a while."

MacDermott studied Bolan a moment longer, and then leaned forward and tapped his smoke into a beanbag ashtray. "Yeah, I'm sure it does. Okay, so you're not on the lam and you ain't done nothing to be guilty for, and that's good enough for me. You see, I trust my people and expect loyalty in return. Who sent you?"

"A guy named Buck Nordstrom."

MacDermott took another long drag and then stubbed out his

smoke in the overflowing ashtray. "Yeah, Nordstrom's a pretty good guy for a Swede. Not much for inside milling, but he's a hell of a powder monkey."

Bolan recognized the term for an explosives man. "Done a bit of that myself in times past."

"Oh, yeah? When's that?"

"Military."

MacDermott nodded, but it didn't seem to impress him one way or another. "Well, afraid I got no use for another explosives guy. How you think you could handle a position as a chaser?"

"Sorry, not up on these logging terms yet."

"You'd work on the yarding line…that's basically where they bring the logs into the mill here. You'd be responsible for disconnecting the chokers and seeing the logs get onto the right conveyers. It's a tough job, but it's what I got and you look big enough to handle it."

"I'll give it a shot."

"Fine, pal, that'll be just fine." He lit another cigarette before adding, "How you want to be paid?"

"I prefer cash," Bolan said.

That brought a smile to MacDermott's face. "You know what? I do, too! You're hired."

Bolan stood with him. "Just like that?"

"Just like that," MacDermott said. "You'll find I'm firm but fair. You'll hear a lot of those in the yard call me Mad Mac. I know about it, and it don't mean nothing, just a bit o' harmless fun on their parts. But they don't do it to my face. You show me respect—I'll show you respect. You see?"

Bolan nodded.

MacDermott came around the desk and crossed in front of Bolan to open his office door. "Now, you give your details to Sally out there, and she'll make sure you get on the payroll."

"Okay, but how much?"

"You want to know the pay. Don't worry about that, you'll be well-compensated…more, *much* more than I think you'll be expecting. Just go out and talk to Sally there and she'll take care of you. Okay?"

Bolan decided to play a card and see where it led him. "Can I ask you a question, Mr. MacDermott?"

"Ya can call me Fagan when we're alone, pal."

"Okay. I've heard Mickey Gowan owns this mill. Is that true?"

Something dulled in MacDermott's green eyes, and his expression flattened. A wisp of smoke curled off the cigarette that dangled from his mouth and caught his eye, but his face barely twitched. He studied Bolan for a long time, and the Executioner wondered for a moment if he'd called MacDermott too soon. Then the mill foreman seemed to move past whatever had struck the nerve and clapped Bolan on the back.

"Yeah, that's right. Mr. Gowan owns this mill, but I'm the push. Ya take your orders from me, mind your p's and q's and you'll be fine. We straight?"

"Yes, sir," Bolan said. "I just wondered, is all."

MacDermott nodded and then waved Bolan out the door.

After he gave his cover credentials to the blond named Sally, Bolan's escorts reappeared and took him out the same way they came in. They left the mill and stopped at the yarding line, where one of the pair gave him a brief rundown of what he'd be doing, introduced him to the only other chaser they had and then led him to his car. Bolan had no doubt they had thoroughly searched it in his absence, but he gave no hint he knew it.

"Be here tomorrow at six o'clock sharp," one of the men instructed.

Bolan drove out of the mill and as soon as he topped the hill just beyond the front gate, the Executioner reached for the cell phone on his belt. He dialed Johnny, who answered immediately.

"I'm in," the Executioner said. He gave his brother the address.

Bolan listened to the clack of a keyboard for a moment, then Johnny said, "Yeah, Mickey Gowan definitely owns that mill."

"Wouldn't surprise me if he owned the whole town," Bolan replied. "You find anything else connecting him to the ELF?"

"He's funneling money through every business in the region. And what he's bringing in doesn't come close to matching the revenues for his business holdings. Weird thing is, Gowan has a lot of business holdings but all of this just comes down to a paper trail. In other words, a lot of unknown money coming into these businesses but very little goes out."

"Sounds like money laundering."

Johnny grunted assent.

Bolan continued, "What you've described to me sounds a lot like a reverse pyramid scheme."

"What do you mean?"

"Gowan's got business everywhere, most likely paper companies. He gets the common folks to invest, whether it be real estate, small-business buy-ins, stocks…whatever. He promises the money will come back but it never does. In this case, the average citizen around here doesn't have the kind of money we're talking about."

"But an organization like the ELF would," Johnny concluded.

"Yeah. I think Gowan's taking their cash and running out on them. The ELF thinks it has funds to draw from so they increase activities. Unfortunately, they're not likely to see a dime of it back, since nobody can really tie the Gowan Family directly to the money, so the ELF takes it out on innocent citizens who signed actual receivership."

"Okay, but why shoot down military aircraft?"

"Military bases mean jobs for the surrounding communities," Bolan said. "Put those bases on alert or attack private corporations and you decrease revenues. Ultimately, it adds up to unnecessary bloodshed and a breakdown in economic surplus."

"That's a hell of a way to stick it to the common man."

"It's also disastrous to public safety."

"What's your plan?"

"It sounds like it's time to shake things up. I think I know where to start. I'll be in touch."

Bolan disconnected the call and drove into downtown Timber

Vale. The streets were crowded with vehicles and an equal amount of foot traffic. He made a couple of passes before turning onto a side street and proceeding to an alleyway that ran along the back of a strip mall. He parked his rental in a discreet area and went EVA.

Something nagged at the back of his mind, but he couldn't put his finger on it. He ran through the events since his arrival. None of this added up. If Gowan had his fingers into all of the local businesses and was making cash hand-over-fist from them, it wouldn't encourage the guy to turn on the ELF. Even ecoterrorists knew how it worked. Gowan stood to make a lot more money from the local business trades in this area than he did from the cash holdings of a few small-time domestic terrorist outfits. It only made sense the ELF would focus its efforts on the local businesses if it discovered it was losing money. No, there had to be more to it than that. This town bothered him, as well. Things were almost *too* perfect here; everybody was friendly, willing to lend a stranger a helping hand. Men like Bolan still believed in the general goodness and charity of humankind, but that didn't mean he took everything at face value. Some things required a closer, deeper inspection—the Executioner just couldn't be sure where to focus his efforts.

And then it dawned on him: the waitress! She looked vaguely familiar to him, but he couldn't figure why. Then he remembered he'd seen her before, earlier in the week at Tulelake at the FBI offices where Kellogg worked. She looked a lot older as a waitress, the heavier makeup and the world-weary expression, but he couldn't forget the eyes. Bolan walked along the side of the building and crossed the street to the diner. A Closed sign hung on the door with a hand-scrawled note that read, "Sorry, Earl out sick."

Not likely. He'd seen Earl just a few hours before and the guy looked fine.

Bolan cupped his hand to the door and peered inside; he saw a fleeting movement in back—something like two people struggling—and then descended from the narrow stoop and circled around back. He found a rear door marked for deliveries only and tried it. It opened without trouble. Bolan stuck his head into the semidark interior. He could hear angry voices inside, male voices, followed by a feminine yelp of pain.

The Executioner kicked it into high gear, opening the door just enough to slip inside as he brought the Beretta into play. He left the door ajar enough to let the morning sunlight illuminate his way and moved through the storage room to a set of swing doors. He cracked one enough to see two men standing with their backs to him. They were holding the waitress in check, and Bolan arrived just in time to see a third man slap her across the face.

Bolan shouldered through the swing doors and raised the Beretta. In a hard, cold voice he said, "Fun's over, boys."

One of the pair holding the waitress turned and emitted a yelp of surprise. The other stupidly clawed for something in the front of his pants. Bolan didn't bother to see what it was. He leveled the sound-suppressed pistol nearly point-blank at the man's head and squeezed the trigger. The subsonic cartridge let out a report not much louder than a cough, and the thug's head immediately disappeared in a crimson spray of bone and brain matter. A large chunk splattered the side of his cohort's face.

The second guy stumbled back and fumbled for his own weapon. The Executioner helped him along with a front kick that sent him reeling. The hood's arms windmilled in an attempt to maintain his balance, but the momentum eventually got the better of him. He crashed into a side counter and brought a full plastic tray of silverware onto his head.

The remaining assailant went for cover, and Bolan saw the glint of light on metal in his hand. Bolan rushed forward and pulled the waitress out of the way just in time to prevent her from being struck by any of the five wild shots the gunman sent in her direction. He shoved her not too gently through the swing doors as he leveled the Beretta 93-R in the enemy's direction and snapped off a pair of shots to keep the guy's head down.

Bolan followed after the waitress and gestured toward the door as she recovered from his rough shove. "Head out the back."

"What the hell are you doing here?"

"Later. Now go," he ordered.

She started to put her hands on her hips and stand there defiantly, but Bolan didn't give her the chance to argue. He grabbed her arm and assisted her to the back, pushing her through the door with his bodyweight as he kept facing forward in anticipation the gunman would follow. The guy did just as Bolan predicted and burst through the swing doors. He leveled his Beretta and squeezed the trigger even as the gunman snapped off a shot of his own. The 9 mm round punched through the thug's chest in a bloody spray, and the impact knocked him through the door. The shot he triggered went high above Bolan's head and lodged in the wood frame of the doorway.

The Executioner emerged into the narrow alleyway in time to see a black SUV round a corner and roar toward them.

4

"Move!"

Bolan shoved the waitress away from the charging SUV and followed on her heels. They ran like hell and rounded the corner of the building in time to avoid being run down. Bolan heard the tires grind to a stop on the broken asphalt and crushed gravel of the alleyway, followed by the reports of automatic-weapons fire.

Louise emitted a sudden cry and stumbled, but Bolan caught her before she fell and helped her along the sidewalk. They reached the cover of the building front and then raced across the street. Bolan released her arm when he sensed she regained her balance. He took the lead and commanded her to follow him to his car.

As they climbed into the rental simultaneously and closed the doors, Bolan quipped, "Friends of yours?"

"I thought about asking you the same question," she shot back.

Bolan bit off a reply as he peeled out to a side street, leaving hot rubber on the pavement. The SUV rolled up on their tail in no time flat. Bolan's eyes flicked to the rearview mirror, then he glanced at the waitress. He didn't fail to notice the very nice pair of legs that emerged from the skirt of her uniform. Not the legs of a middle-aged woman. From that distance he could also see there weren't the usual facial wrinkles, which left him to deduce she wasn't in her forties as he'd originally guessed.

"That's a good makeup job," he said. "Your FBI contacts have real talent."

"You know who I am?" she asked, although she expressed only mild surprise.

Bolan nodded. "I recognized you from the field office in Siskiyou County."

"I recognized you, too," she said. "That's why I'd hoped you poke around for a few days, get bored and leave."

"Funny way of showing it," Bolan replied. "Think you can handle the wheel?"

The back windows shattered under the impact of fresh autofire before she could answer. Glass shards rained onto the pair, but fortunately didn't injure either of them. When Bolan did a closer inspection of his occupant, however, he noticed her bleeding from her right arm. She'd probably been grazed back at the restaurant when they were fleeing on foot.

"I can do better than that," she said. "Give me your gun."

"What?"

"Your pistol."

Bolan shook his head curtly. "No dice."

"Listen, mister, I'm grateful for all your help, but this is FBI business."

"It's my business," Bolan said but on afterthought he decided to hand over his Beretta. "Okay, I'll drive, you shoot."

"Such a gentleman," she teased.

She twisted until her knees were in the seat and faced rearward. Bolan could see her level the pistol, expertly using a modified Weaver's grip, her forearms braced on the top edge of the seat to the right of the headrest. A moment later, she squeezed the trigger three times in rapid succession. She followed that with a second volley.

Bolan watched in his rearview mirror as the SUV swerved to avoid the shots. The first volley left sparks on the grille but didn't appear to have any effect. The latter triburst spiderwebbed the windshield, effectively blocking the driver's field of vision, and Bolan noticed the passenger's side spattered with red. Obviously one of the woman's shots had scored. The Executioner decided to take advantage of the driver's obscured sight. He rolled down the passenger's side window and grabbed hold of his new ally as he slammed on the brakes and steered into the deserted oncoming lane.

The SUV shot past them.

Bolan snatched the pistol from the woman as he accelerated and ordered her to take cover. He came parallel with the SUV and thumbed the selector to 3-round bursts before squeezing the trigger. The slide ratcheted obediently—extracted one casing after another—as the warrior put three 9 mm Parabellum rounds in the driver. The SUV swerved off the road, jumped the curb and collided with a massive pine tree. Bolan didn't even slow down when the engine ignited. They were more than two blocks away when they heard the rumble of an explosion.

"Damn!" the waitress said. "Pretty nice work, mister!"

"Not bad yourself," Bolan replied. "Now, let's find some place to talk."

THE PLACE ENDED UP being a forest preserve about sixteen miles outside Timber Vale. Bolan didn't mind the drive. It gave both of them time to decompress while affording him the advantage to watch for tails. Once convinced no one followed, he turned onto a road indicated by his companion, stopped in a shaded area near a small lake and killed the engine.

"You want to explain what happened back there?" Bolan asked.

She wrinkled her nose at him. "Not much for small talk, are you?"

"Not when someone's trying to kill me."

"You're of no interest to them," she said. "Besides, you don't have anything to worry about. I'll protect you."

"I'll bet."

"So what do you want to know?"

"Let's start with your real name, because I'm pretty sure it isn't Louise."

She extended a hand and replied, "Special Agent Sandra Newbury, FBI. I'm here on temporary assignment."

"And your handler," Bolan interjected. "I bet his name's Kellogg."

"How'd you know?"

"Same reason I knew you worked for the FBI," Bolan said. "I recognized you when I was there."

She laughed—a nice laugh. "Guess I'm getting sloppy."

"Guess so. What's Kellogg have you doing up here?"

"It's a long story."

Bolan frowned. "I have time."

Newbury blew out a breath through pursed lips, then laid her head against the headrest and stared at the lake. "I was assigned here by Washington. I'm what they call a flip. I travel a lot, take undercover cases and then once the job's done I move on. I specialize in fitting into particular areas or groups, but I'm never in for any long-term gigs. You probably hear or even know of the ones who go under for months and months, many times even years, and then after that they do regular fieldwork."

Bolan nodded. He'd known many in the law-enforcement community who did such work—even a few he counted as friends.

"Anyway, I was assigned to get inside the Timber Vale community," Newbury continued. "It's gone a lot longer than maybe it should have. We've long suspected corruption by organized-crime elements up in this neck of the woods, and what I've seen in recent weeks makes me think more and more we're right."

"You're talking about Mickey Gowan and clan."

"Right again! Sounds like you know your way around here. You work for Washington also?"

Bolan shook his head. "No, but we'll get into that later. Right now, I need to know everything you can tell me about Gowan's operations up here."

"Afraid I can't tell you much," Newbury replied with a shrug. "Especially since I don't even know who you work for or your clearance level."

"Much higher than yours. I'm afraid you'll have to trust me

on that and everything else I tell you. I don't have any credentials with me to prove what I'm saying, not that I feel I have to."

"Then what makes you think I should cooperate with you?"

"Mainly because I saved your tail back there," Bolan countered. "That should be enough proof I'm on your side."

Newbury's resolve seemed to melt some, as did her defensive expression. "I suppose I do owe you one on that count. How about at least a name?"

"I gave it to you last night. Cooper."

Newbury nodded. "Cooper it is, although I'm betting it's a cover. Anyway, it was just luck of the draw you came along when you did. Thanks."

"Luck had nothing to do with it. I'd planned to follow up on a lead I got with you, once I realized who you were and where I'd seen you before."

"A lead on what?"

"About a week ago, a pair of F-15s was shot down at Kingsley Airfield."

Newbury nodded and said evenly, "I heard about that. My brother happens to be a pilot for the Texas Air National Guard. I'm a little more sensitive when I hear about those kinds of things. It reminds me just how short life is."

"It can be," Bolan replied.

"But I thought that was ruled an accident," she said.

"That's what they're telling the press. In reality, we think the Earth Liberation Front might have been responsible."

"Doesn't sound like their MO. And besides, what does any of this have to do with Mickey Gowan and my case?" she asked.

"I'm coming to that. My intelligence on Gowan shows he's funneling monies through the local businesses all along this region for the ELF. Giving them a place to store their cash, launder funds, the works. Neither the Justice Department nor the IRS would look hard at a community of this size, particularly if the growth rate wasn't significant. Timber Vale's the perfect place for Gowan's operations."

"Okay, but for what purpose? If Gowan allows the businesses around here to get hurt, that's only going to look bad on him."

"Not if he's using those business to pipeline cash but making the individual business owners sign receivership," Bolan said. "Think about it. He fronts the ELF's money to the business owners. He can show those as legitimate business transactions to the ELF, make them think he's doing it to protect their funds. Then somebody defaults and he lets it get back to the ELF the receivers have stolen the money. The ELF then takes it out on the individuals and Gowan gets away squeaky clean with the embezzled funds."

"And after it's over, he then comes in and restores the thing at a quarter of the cost," Newbury concluded. "Nobody's the wiser!"

"Right."

Newbury looked at Bolan with utter surprise. "It's ingenious if true."

"That's a big if right now," Bolan admitted. "What I need is some corroborating evidence. And I need you to help me get it."

"How?"

"Keep doing what you've been doing," he said.

"That'll be tougher now that Gowan's people are onto me," Newbury replied.

"Those weren't Gowan's people," Bolan replied. "They were too well-trained and -equipped. Gowan's men are thugs and hoods, nothing more. Those guys weren't maybe the brightest of the bunch, but they were definitely experts in their field."

"But why would the ELF come after me?"

Bolan had to admit he didn't have an answer to that question. He didn't have any proof the men who attacked Newbury weren't from Gowan, but his instinct told him otherwise and Bolan always listened to it. No, those men were after more than the rent money.

"What kind of questions did they ask?"

"They wanted to know where Earl was, who owned the place…stuff like that."

"Mickey Gowan doesn't own that restaurant?"

She shook her head. "Too small. I actually got hired there by Earl about two months back. Earl did all the resupply, ordered things whenever I asked him, signed all the checks. I just assumed Earl owned the place, so I figured it was a good place to keep my cover while I poked into other business ventures."

"I know Gowan owns the mill," Bolan said.

Newbury nodded. "As well as the mercantile, bank and just about everything else in Timber Vale. He doesn't do much with the small businesses, but he's got his teeth into all the major capital ventures."

"Good," the Executioner said with a nod. "I'll need a list of those as soon as you can get them to me."

Newbury batted her eyelashes and said, "Still not going to tell me who you work for?"

Bolan shook his head. "No, and I'd appreciate if you don't ask me anymore."

"Fine," she said. She folded her arms and said, "So what now?"

"You have someplace safe you can go?"

She nodded. "I can wait at a friend's house until Kellogg gets up here."

"Not good," Bolan said. "I don't trust Kellogg, and I think it's better if you don't contact him."

"He's my handler," Newbury protested. "I *have* to call him."

"I don't trust Kellogg," he repeated.

Newbury sighed. "You think he's in bed with Gowan."

"Yeah. You?"

Something in Newbury's eyes betrayed she had similar feelings. Bolan had wondered why the inaction on Kellogg's part.

"I don't have a shred of proof but…well, I've suspected for some time. It's hard not to get a pretty clear picture of what's going on in smaller communities like Siskiyou County or up here in Timber Vale. Kellogg knows a lot of people, and he seems to have trouble keeping a low profile."

"Likes to be in the limelight," Bolan cut in.

"Exactly. And when you mention you don't trust him, then

that just seems to confirm my own suspicions and tells me I'm not crazy."

"So for now I'd say keep quiet and don't rattle too many cages," Bolan said as he started the car.

"We're leaving?"

"I'll drop you off at my motel, and then I've got a few more things to take care of before I start work tomorrow morning at the mill."

Newbury scratched at her head and finally yanked off her wig in unceremonious fashion. Bolan could see the cause of her discomfort. She'd used an assortment of rubber bands and metal clips to wind her dark hair against her head. She began to pull them loose one by one as Bolan pulled onto the road.

"So you convinced MacDermott to give you a job."

"You know him, eh?"

She nodded. "He comes into the diner all the time."

"You trust him?"

"Hell no!" Newbury popped a stick of gum in her mouth before adding, "Mac's a braggart and a loudmouth. He's also known for tipping them back a little too often." She made a drinking gesture.

"That should prove helpful," Bolan said. "Heavy drinking's a weakness. Maybe I can use it to get under his skin."

"Just be careful you don't get too deep," she said.

"I can take care of myself."

"Maybe…but keep your eyes open anyway. The MacDermott fan club has quite a membership."

"Is he on Gowan's payroll?"

"Better believe it." Newbury completed the task of removing the hair restraints. She tossed her head back and forth and lowered the window, and her long, thick strands of red-brown hair blew easily under the high-speed breezes.

Bolan thought he smelled something like apples or strawberries, but the scent quickly faded. "What's his angle?"

"Mac's a piece of work. I know he resents working under Mickey Gowan. He's been heard mouthing off about that more than once. I know he went toe-to-toe with one of Gowan's right-hand men a few months back, a guy by the name of Billy Moran."

"Yeah, Moran's no longer with us."

Newbury looked at Bolan in shock. From her expression she knew good and well what Bolan meant by the comment. He looked for something more there, but he didn't get anything. He still had no real reason to trust Newbury, but for now he only needed her for information.

"Like I said," Newbury said more quietly, "Mac hits the sauce pretty often and pretty hard. And he likes his women, too. Considers himself somewhat of a ladies' man. He's even hit on me a few times at the restaurant. Usually it's after the bars close and he's been out most of the night. I always just tell him I have a boyfriend and that seems to satisfy him."

"Well, if you need somebody to actually stand in for the part, give me a call."

Newbury burst into laughter. "You know, that's about the most gentlemanly offer I've had in quite a while. Say, you mind if I ask you something?"

Bolan shook his head.

"This other business you have to do. What exactly is it?"

Bolan considered the question a moment and then shrugged. "When I went to the mill for my little job interview this morning, some of MacDermott's guys searched my vehicle. I expected they would, so I didn't leave anything incriminating inside of it. Still, that tells me they're up to something. I need to find out what it is, make sure if I get chummy with this MacDermott I'm not going to get blindsided."

"Okay, sure, but what exactly are you going to do?" Newbury pressed.

"Simple. I'm going to do exactly what they're hoping I'll do," Bolan said.

"Which is?"

"Pick a fight."

5

Jeff Kellogg never believed in putting his eggs all in one basket, which included the basket of the Gowan Family. Kellogg knew his only chance of emerging unscathed should Gowan get caught with his hands in the till would be to provide as much critical information to Gowan's enemies as possible. Of course, information didn't come cheap, and Kellogg took a distinct pleasure in double-dipping. Kellogg's benefactor was a man who, according to his FBI profile, headed up the local chapter of the Earth Liberation Front.

Many who knew him described Percy Jeter as an outgoing and personable man—not a surprise considering he operated as head of the Western States Campgrounds for Challenged Youth. Jeter's work with the WSCCY afforded him complete autonomy and discretion; after all, he had a lot of old money and influence backing him, not to mention assistance from the federal and state governments. That kind of wealth and power practically immunized him from prosecution, and most people didn't give a tinker's damn about his political affiliations.

The very thought of it sickened Kellogg, but the profit motive allowed him to find a way to see beyond the pettiness of it all.

Kellogg had specifically requested they meet in a popular park just outside Tulelake. He knew about Jeter's secret location in the mountainous terrain surrounding Siskiyou Pass, but he didn't like to meet there. Kellogg preferred neutral territory, and since Jeter liked his privacy and obviously didn't trust Kellogg, he usually sent some lackey. This time though, Jeter had come himself.

The two men sat across from each other at a picnic table. The result of years of cushy living off tax-free donations lent Percy Jeter a groomed, distinguished appearance. Legally, Jeter received very little in the way of income, but he lived like a king. Nobody looked too hard, though, as he provided a number of services through the WSCCY, a not-for-profit cash cow. Salt-and-pepper hair and beard complemented the tanned skin and clear blue eyes that jutted from under pronounced orbits.

"To what do I owe the pleasure this time?" Jeter asked in a deep voice.

"We got to talk about what happened last week," Kellogg said. He looked around. Nobody seemed to pay attention to them. Families played together, parents pushing kids on swings or feeding ducks or just enjoying a picnic, and joggers and cyclists took advantage of the nice day as they traveled along the gravel paths that skirted the park.

Jeter shrugged. "What's to talk about?"

"How about what went down at Kingsley Airfield?"

"I don't know what you're talking about."

Kellogg waved the flat of his palm as he countered, "Don't be coy, Percy. You know damned well what I'm talking about. Why the fuck are you shooting down American fighter jets? That's not your style."

Jeter leaned forward in a menacing fashion. "That's exactly my style. You promised to rein in Mickey Gowan, and nothing. You promised to protect our assets, and nothing. You promised we wouldn't have to worry about outside interference while we build up our cash reserves, and nothing. We've paid you a lot of money, Kellogg, and you haven't done a single goddamned thing."

"I've done a lot."

"Bullshit. You've collected from us *and* from Gowan, and I haven't seen you do one thing to earn your keep so far. Well, the free ride's over and it's out of my hands. The Committee decided."

There he went with his mysterious talk of the Committee. Allegedly, the Committee acted as the unofficial head of the Earth Liberation Front. It was chaired by some lackey who oversaw a handful of lackeys, one of them being Jeter, and who allegedly administered the entire western region from Washington to California and extending as far east as the Continental Divide.

"You can stop paying me if you want, but I can just about guarantee that I'm the least of your worries right now."

Jeter didn't look convinced. "Yeah, right."

"Blow it off, then. But just remember that Gowan's going to continue robbing you blind, and the small amount you're paying me is a pittance compared to the millions of dollars you're going to lose if you continue to trust him."

"Maybe we just plan to rub him out of the picture entirely," Jeter said.

Kellogg let out a snort. "Sure…whatever you say. The FBI's been after him for years and they still haven't come up with squat."

"We're not the FBI."

"No, you're not. And I think that's the first thing we've agreed on since we formed this little partnership. Listen, it's none of my business how you screw this up for you and your precious Committee, but I'm sure as a hell not going to let you screw it up for me."

Jeter sighed. "You still haven't told me why you called this meeting."

"I came to tell you about the return on your investment," Kellogg said. "All that money you think you wasted on me is about to pay off."

"And how's that?"

Kellogg couldn't resist the urge to grin in triumph. "Gowan's got trouble brewing in his own backyard and he doesn't even know it. There's a town not too far from Kingsley, Timber Vale. You know it?"

"Of course I know it. We've funneled a good amount of our funds through Gowan's businesses there. So tell me what I don't know."

"That town basically lives and dies by the mill. If that thing were to close down, Gowan would lose his ass because it ties into every other business he's got his claws into."

Jeter made a show of yawning.

"I know you know all that," Kellogg continued. "But what you don't know is that Gowan's foreman up there, a guy named Mac-Dermott, he's basically acting as the union head. And he's got a real hard-on for the likes of Mickey Gowan."

"They don't like each other," Jeter said, cocking his head slightly.

"It's worse than that. MacDermott hates Gowan's guts and there's talk of a coup."

"When?"

"Soon," Kellogg replied. "In fact, sooner than you might want to believe. Within the week is what I'd assume. Now, when Mac-Dermott makes his move it's going to get bloody. And if Mac-Dermott manages to take over, that's going to free Gowan's hold on things and then you can just move right in and get all the money back you lost."

"What about this MacDermott?"

Kellogg shrugged. "What about him? The guy's a dumb-ass, for one. Two, I can guarantee he doesn't know the first thing about how Gowan's been soaking you guys. So what you take he isn't going to miss. But you've got just one hitch."

"Uh-oh, here it comes. I should have seen this coming."

"There's a guy who's been poking his nose all around here, name of Cooper. I don't know what official sanctions he's got or if he even has government ties. Might be a freelancer. But he's all over Gowan right now, and he seems to have a line on quite a number of the juicier details on Gowan's business. Worse, I think he might be responsible for taking out Gowan's main guy, Billy Moran."

"I heard about Moran," Jeter admitted. "We chalked it up to simple infighting."

"Shows what the hell you know," Kellogg countered. "And demonstrates just once more why you pay me—to make sure you get the right intel."

Jeter splayed his hands. "Okay, so maybe you know a couple things we don't. So what? I still don't see what the hell any of this has to do with the fact that Mickey Gowan and crew are now into us for about six million."

"It has everything to do with it. If Cooper manages to put this thing down before you can get control of it yourself, you'll never see that six million again. I don't know what Cooper's aim is but I'm sure of one thing. He isn't doing this for money."

"Shouldn't be difficult to take out one guy," Jeter said.

Kellogg nodded. "Agreed. Bear in mind he's already putting down roots in Timber Vale."

"Well, then, we'll just have to make sure he doesn't outstay his welcome."

BY 1600, THINGS at Backcut were getting into full swing.

It almost seemed cliché to Bolan they would have a place like this for the lumber workers after their shift. Most of the occupants Bolan recalled seeing on his minitour through the mill early that morning. Backcut had a full-service bar and eatery complete with a jukebox system for happy hour and live entertainment starting nightly at 8:00 p.m. The place had become party central for most of Timber Vale's residents, and Bolan figured the best place to stir up the natives would be where the natives spent most of their leisure time. They would be especially susceptible here with food, liquor and music to chase away the cares of the day.

Using his best working-man saunter, Bolan made his way to the long bar of polished, knotty wood. He ordered a beer in a longneck bottle and then found a place at the bar a few seats from none other than Fagan MacDermott. It hadn't been terribly difficult to pick him out of a crowd—that boisterous brogue accent getting louder with the obvious liquor in him—and the collection of mill bosses cloistered around him. What a pack of hyenas, this crew.

Bolan sat and watched the tirades, the joking and punching of arms and slapping of backs until he could hardly stand to watch anymore. He wanted to approach MacDermott at the man's most disadvantaged, and watching him drink at that pace

Bolan knew it wouldn't take long. It didn't. After another hour, Bolan barely finished with his beer, a couple of men headed toward the bathrooms, which left a comfortable two still hanging on MacDermott's every word.

Bolan downed the last of his beer but brought the bottle along as he slid from the bar stool and walked to where the trio perched. One of the men stood leaning against the bar, MacDermott and the remaining tough occupied barstools.

Bolan tossed a casual salute. "Hey, boys."

MacDermott turned in surprise and his expression froze a moment, perplexed, then he broke into one of those toothy grins. Bolan quickly assessed the threesome. MacDermott had obviously consumed quite a bit of whatever he'd been drinking from a frosted mug. The man standing seemed pretty straight, but the one seated next to MacDermott—one of the two who'd escorted him through the mill that morning—swayed a bit on the barstool and blinked at Bolan with bloodshot eyes.

"Well!" MacDermott exclaimed. "Cooper, me boy! Buy a drink?"

"No, thanks." Bolan gestured with his bottle. "I'm good."

MacDermott looked at his two counterparts and then all three men burst into laughter.

Bolan rendered a sheepish smile although privately he knew what engendered such an outburst. MacDermott hadn't been asking if he could buy Bolan a drink, but rather insinuated Bolan should be the one to buy…for all of them, most likely. But the Executioner knew if he wanted to get inside the circle he had to play dumb. He'd pushed a bit hard earlier in the day asking about Mickey Gowan; now was the time to act a bit more nonchalant. At least until the timing worked and he could really speak his mind.

The laughter died quickly when MacDermott's smile melted into a frown. He continued, a bit drunkenly, "I'm hurt, Coop. I figured a guy like you for one o' the smart ones. That's why I hired ya."

"I'm the same guy now as I was this morning," Bolan replied, trying for his best smile.

MacDermott's drunken companion spoke up now. "You sound like a bit of a smart-mouth, sonny." The term amused Bolan as he guessed to have ten years or better on the ruffian. "You ought to talk a bit nicer to ol' Mac here."

"I wasn't talking bad to him," Bolan said. "And I'm pretty sure I wasn't talking to you at all. And while we're on the subject, I don't recognize you. I recognize your friend here that escorted me to Mac's office. But you I haven't met before. Maybe you were one of the guys who searched my car."

A stunned silence fell over all three men, and Bolan measured the looks of awe on their respective faces. Obviously, they hadn't known he was on to them. And Bolan knew, as they did, the only reason for them to search would be if they suspected he was the law or one of Gowan's boys. It was time to make his move while he had them off guard.

Bolan chuckled and waved his hand. "It's okay, though. I know what's going on. I heard through the grapevine about the trouble with Mickey Gowan."

MacDermott raised an eyebrow. "You mentioned that this morning, too. You know Mickey?"

"Not personally. But I know of him and who doesn't? He practically runs this town, and I'm pretty sure he runs the mill. But I'm not working for him if that's what you're worried about. I'm just looking for some honest labor."

"Then you know Mac here's the head of the union," the drunken bootlicker boasted.

"Shut up, Chep," interjected his sober companion. The guy then stepped forward, putting his body between MacDermott and Bolan. He stood approximately the same height as Bolan but easily carried an extra forty pounds. That didn't interest the Executioner as much as how the guy moved, which made the real difference.

The man continued, "We're really not interested in whatever it is you're selling, guy." He jerked his head in the general direction of the bar's exterior wall and said, "You'll need to prove yourself out there before you can impress us with a few keen observations."

"And where exactly," Bolan asked in a mimic of the man's gesture, "is out there?"

"On the yarding line at the mill."

Bolan nodded. "I'll keep that in mind. In the meantime, you guys can skip looking any harder at me. If you want to know something, just ask. No need to pry."

"We'll do like we please!" Chep Flannery stated.

Bolan expressed frostiness. "I don't think so."

The man in front of Bolan reached up to shove him backward, but instead Bolan caught his wrist in a viselike grip and twisted down and out. As the tough yelped in pain, Bolan swung the beer bottle he'd been holding up between them and clipped the man neatly under the jaw. Blood sprayed along the fringes of the man's mouth as he bit his tongue and fractured a couple of teeth. Bolan continued his downward pressure on the man's wrist until he'd maxed him out and then swung the arm out with enough force to flip the man onto the ground.

Flannery started to get up from his stool at the same time as he reached for Bolan, a very unwise move as it put him well off balance. Bolan twisted sideways and then delivered a low, swift kick to the legs of the barstool. The front-stool legs left the ground and sent Flannery backward, arms windmilling, to strike his head on the edge of the bar. Stool and occupant both clattered noisily to the ground.

The two men who'd left a minute earlier now returned and started to accost Bolan, but MacDermott put up a hand. "Hold it! Leave 'im alone…*they* started it. And it looks like old Coop here finished it."

The pair backed off.

MacDermott climbed off his stool in a huff and waved Bolan to a nearby table. The pair sat down, and at that point Bolan called for a fresh bottled beer and one of whatever MacDermott was drinking. The row up front blew over rather quickly, especially when the others could see Flannery and Brutus were going to be okay as the other pair of MacDermott's goons helped them to their feet.

"So let's cut all this bullshit," MacDermott said after the drinks arrived. "What's your real interest in Mickey?"

"Not my interest," Bolan replied. He added, "Interest of some friends of mine. He owes them some money."

MacDermott nodded. "It figures. It was Gowan's idea to actually make me the head of the mill and the union. Between ourselves, the guy ain't got a lick of sense. How much he into you for?"

"Like I said, he doesn't owe me anything. But the people he does owe, well let's just say they're pretty important people. And word has it they'll take apart your nice little town here if they don't see their money real soon."

"Why our town? We ain't done nothing to them."

"Well, that's the funny part." Bolan paused to look around, just to help sell the story, and then lowered his voice to a conspiratorial whisper. "You see, there's no such thing as free money. Especially not all that cash Gowan's been waving at the locals here to get their businesses off the ground. That money doesn't belong to him."

MacDermott nodded in understanding. Drunk as he was, he wasn't stupid. "It belongs to your, ah, 'friends,' as you called them."

"Right."

"So what's that got to do with the rest of us?"

"Well, that's just the thing. I ran into some guys today who were squeezing that waitress over at the diner."

"Louise?" MacDermott's face went red. "They were manhandling Louise? I'll wring their necks!"

"Settle down," Bolan said. "I already took care of them. But I can tell you they were pretty serious and I think they were some of Gowan's guys."

"Well, then, the joke's on them."

"Why?"

MacDermott laughed loudly and then slapped the table. "Because before too much longer we're going to have a strike. And one that Gowan can't do nothing about. Then I'm going to talk him into selling the place to me, as I'm the only one that can keep these people in line. And then we'll be out from under Gowan's thumb."

"Won't probably hurt your pocket too much, either," Bolan noted.

MacDermott expressed devilish intent and lowered his voice. "Of course not, but we ought to just keep that between ourselves."

"You think we can help each other."

"I *definitely* think we can," MacDermott replied.

MacDermott took the bait exactly as Bolan expected. Now all he had to do was wait to spring the trap.

6

Bolan pushed open the motel door and stepped over the threshold. He immediately noticed Newbury's hand hovered near her clutch purse on the nightstand.

"Relax," he said. "And don't shoot me."

She grinned. "I'll try not to hit any vital organs if I do."

"Much appreciated."

"You're scowling. No luck?"

"This is concentration, not scowling," he countered as he closed the door and bolted it before collapsing into a chair. "In fact, I got everything I wanted. It just wasn't what I wanted to hear."

"You talked to Mac?"

Bolan nodded. "It was an interesting chat."

"Then why the long face?"

Bolan sighed and looked at the ceiling before replying, "Don't like what's on the horizon. You're right about no love lost between MacDermott and Gowan. MacDermott told me he's going to stage a coup disguised as a labor dispute."

"So?" Newbury replied with a shrug. "I'd like to think we still live in a country where they'd happily pin a medal on anybody who stood up to a slimeball like Mickey Gowan."

"That's not what concerns me."

Newbury frowned and furrowed her eyebrows. "Then, um, I guess I'm being a bit thick here. I don't understand the problem."

"Gowan's sunk a lot of money into MacDermott and the mill business. I think he's using it to protect his assets. The same ones he's hiding from the ELF. I also think if he finds out it's actually

MacDermott behind this little rebellion, he'll send in the big guns to take care of business. That means a lot of innocent people could get hurt."

"You're right!" Newbury said, now expressing realization at the validity of Bolan's concerns. "If he dispatches a bunch of heavies at the same time the ELF's running their activities, they—"

"Might view it as a challenge," Bolan finished.

"That could start a full-scale war right here in Timber Vale!"

Bolan stood and shoved his hands in his pockets. "Gowan and the ELF are close to blows now. It wouldn't take much to provoke either side."

"I've been thinking about what happened to us earlier," Newbury said after chewing on her lip in silence. "I think that muscle we encountered this morning may have been Gowan's men after all."

"Based on what?"

"Just seems like I've seen one of them before. I couldn't swear to it, but I recall he might have been nosing around town a few months back."

"Well, I'll need to know for sure. Any way you can run him down?"

"Probably, but I'll need access to the FBI's resources. It's time you got me back to my own place."

"I'm not sure it's safe yet," Bolan replied.

As Newbury slid off the bed and into her sandals, she said, "Look, Cooper, I understand you're trying to help. But frankly I have a job to do just like you. And if Kellogg's on the wrong side of this thing I don't want to get shot in the back because I didn't take time to get my head into what's happening here in Shangri-La. If my handler or anyone else in that office is in bed with Gowan, it's my duty to blow it wide open. And seeing as how it's *my* neck on the line where that's concerned, we can agree that should be my call, not yours."

Bolan couldn't help but grin. "You finished?"

Newbury appeared to seriously consider his question and then nodded. "Yeah, I've spoken my piece."

"All right," Bolan said. "Get your things and I'll drive you to your car. But whatever you do, don't stay at your apartment."

Newbury grabbed her purse with a deep sigh, cocked her head and eyed him. "Why?"

"Because I guarantee if whoever sent that crew this morning is on to you, they're on to me, too. Neither of us can afford that kind of distraction right now."

"Fine...deal."

Bolan nodded and turned toward the door but never reached the handle. The motel window imploded. The cheap curtains stopped a hail of glass missiles that would have otherwise cut Newbury to shreds. They didn't do anything to stop the bullets, however, as slugs punched through the flimsy material and imbedded themselves in the wall. Bolan hit the ground and turned to see Newbury already there. He then rolled on his side and drew the Beretta, its selector set for 3-round bursts. The firestorm kept up another ten seconds and then died.

Bolan rose to a combat crouch, opened the door and swung his pistol into acquisition while maintaining relative cover behind the doorjamb. His sights fell on the blond passenger of a late-model Corvette. The driver revved the engine impatiently as the blond machine gunner loaded a second clip. He never got time to put the weapon into battery.

Bolan squeezed the trigger and delivered a trio of 9 mm Parabellum slugs. Two rounds ripped the man's neck wide open while the third shattered his jaw. His weapon clattered outside the car while his body slid out of sight.

The tires smoked as the driver put the vehicle into gear and tried to move off. Bolan dispatched front and rear passenger's side tires before the Corvette could gain traction. Rubber shredded from the tires, and instead of moving away the vehicle spun out. The driver was forced to slam on the brakes before the vehicle went completely out of his control. Bolan rushed for the driver as the man attempted to bail. As he got close, he recognized the thug as one of MacDermott's men.

The driver started to reach into his coat on seeing Bolan approach, but the Executioner beat him to the punch. He delivered a front kick that jarred the man's arm loose from the hardware he'd been reaching for, and the pistol skittered across the parking lot.

Bolan grabbed the driver by the shirt and slammed him against the Corvette. He pressed the hot muzzle of the Beretta beneath his chin. "Wrong again."

"Wh-wha—" the guy began.

"You keeping picking fights you can't win," Bolan said. He hardened his expression, the threat implicit in his tone. "Who sent you?"

"You promise not to kill me?"

"You show me the same courtesy?" Bolan asked. "I've got no beef with you. Mac calls a truce and you come gunning for me anyway. Why?"

The driver produced a scowling laugh. "Mac's a small fish in a big pond."

"Who owns the pond?"

"Who do you think?"

Mickey Gowan. Bolan didn't even have to voice it. Someone had put Gowan's men onto both his trail and Sandra Newbury's. Kellogg was the only common denominator in that equation. Not only could he have been the only one to betray Newbury's undercover status to Gowan's thugs, but he'd also more than likely deduced it was Bolan who pulled the trigger on Billy Moran.

Bolan jammed the muzzle tighter against the hood's chin. "Unlike your pal in the car, you've bought a reprieve. It seems your loyalties don't lie with MacDermott."

"You can't prove that."

The Executioner replied with a frosty grin, "I don't have to. You can walk away from trying to kill me if you give me one simple thing."

"I don't think so, pal. I ain't no rat."

"You won't even rate *that* high if I don't get what I want,"

Bolan reminded him with another sharp nudge. "I want Gowan's three top moneymakers in this town."

"The mill makes the most cash."

Bolan shook his head once. "No good. The mill needs to stay in operation…at least for now. What else? Who does Gowan have his hooks into most?"

The hood appeared to consider his options, obviously realized there weren't any and shrugged. What the hell did he care? He was banking on Bolan to keep his promise that he could walk away from it all. The thug in the fancy suit started to talk, and within a minute Bolan had his list.

The Executioner turned to look at Newbury standing behind him and asked, "Sound about right?"

She nodded.

"All right, you can hook him up." Sirens wailed in the night, signaling the rapid approach of the law as Newbury stepped forward, expertly frisked the guy and then put him in handcuffs.

"Where you going?" she asked Bolan, who had started for his vehicle.

"Away," he replied. "I can't risk getting caught up with a lot of questions, especially not right now."

"Well, what the hell am I supposed to tell them?"

"You'll think up a good story," Bolan said as he climbed into his vehicle. He started the engine, rolled down the window and as he passed by her he added, "I'm betting somewhere in that pretty head is one wild imagination."

As Bolan cleared the area, a police cruiser screamed past him, followed a minute later by a sheriff's SUV. Bolan watched both disappear in his rearview mirror. He slowed some on the treacherous winding road as it started to sprinkle. He hated to ditch Newbury like that, but he really couldn't afford to get hung up with the red tape of a police incident. He bet Sandra Newbury could handle the locals and then some.

Bolan had already planned his next move, but now he had the intel to back the play. The entire basis of Gowan's operation in

Timber Vale and the other towns where he prospered came down to two things: money and the best places to hide it. The Executioner figured the ELF probably wasn't the only organization Gowan had stuck it to in the past, but if he had to pick the *wrong* organization to cross, the ELF would be at the top of Bolan's list.

His first target would be an all-night gambling joint known to more than dabble in illegal bookmaking activities. In this case, while gambling was legal in Oregon, such establishments had to be licensed. Gowan seemed to think himself above such requirements. Moreover, this gave him a place to stash a nearly unlimited pile of cash. Bolan meant to liquidate the liquid assets.

The Executioner drove to the downtown area. Timber Vale sported a considerable nightlife for a population under a thousand, and the main drag sported as many lights and colorful storefronts as some of the streets just off the Las Vegas Strip. Bolan counted at least a dozen bars and taverns in the four blocks he covered, peppered with small diners, a drugstore, cleaner and a hardware store. Young people cruised in everything from jalopies and to their dads' convertibles, apparently oblivious to the light rain. One young woman even flashed her breasts for Bolan at a light. Her boyfriend peeled rubber to turn onto a side road, probably more to save his own embarrassment than protect his date's modesty.

Bolan shook his head and proceeded along the street. He took note of the Irish pub that served as a front to Gowan's basement gambling operations. The place seemed laid out similar to the one he'd penetrated in Tulelake, although this one wasn't quite as upscale. At least, he didn't get that impression from the guy who seemed to loiter just outside the entrance. Bolan finally took a side street, parked up the block from the pub so he could keep watch on it with his side mirror while he settled on a battle plan.

He considered the frontal approach simply because it worked, but the increased activity since that morning would definitely have the local police in a heightened state of alert. He figured on an extra measure of vigilance by Gowan's security people, too, since they had obviously identified him as a threat.

Bolan considered other viable scenarios, but he didn't like any of them. There was still too much activity on the street. Finally, after a few more minutes scoping out the target, Bolan started his car and drove away. He'd wait for a more opportune time, maybe when they were shutting down for the night. He decided to proceed to his next target, this one on the other side of the town. When he arrived he found the swanky, upscale neighborhood quiet. Most of its residents were either downtown or had retired for the night.

All except one place, anyway. Bolan pulled to the curb on a side street a block down from the two-story house that sat on nearly an acre of manicured lawns. Clearly it was the largest and most beautiful home in the area, although some of the surrounding homes were just large and nice enough to keep this particular spread from seeming out of place.

The Beretta dangling from shoulder leather, Bolan popped the trunk, retrieved a combat knife and a trio of flash-bang grenades. He didn't figure to encounter much resistance on this one, so he forsook an autorifle for the .44 Magnum Desert Eagle. He wrapped the webbed gunbelt around his waist, clipped the grenades to it and closed the trunk. Then he headed up the street and straight into the arms of the unexpected. Still, the Executioner had a plan, the best kind of strategy.

Strike first, strike hard—and leave the enemy reeling!

7

Bolan had it on good authority the residents inside this house participated in the world's oldest profession. The thug he'd encountered back at the motel also indicated the place was relatively unguarded, watched over by only a few handpicked men under Gowan's chief overseer, whose name the squealer didn't know.

Bolan walked casually along the sidewalk until he reached the front gate. A pair of wrought-iron gates, which swung open remotely, blocked the entrance to the driveway but they were only waist high. Bolan looked around once and then easily vaulted them. He fisted the Beretta and headed toward the house in a crouched run. The numbers would soon start tumbling as he figured the place sported a pretty advanced security system. Bolan nearly reached the front door when the initial resistance appeared in the form of two dark-suited gunmen who seemed to materialize out of the shadows.

Bolan swung the Beretta at the nearer target and triggered a single round that caught the hard case in the gut. The force drove him off his feet and flipped him onto his back. The second gunner had his pistol up and tracking, but he couldn't match the Executioner's fluid, practiced movements. Bolan took him with a double-tap to the chest. The man staggered and continued forward before performing an ungraceful chin skid on the slippery grass.

Bolan approached the front door of the house and rapped his knuckles against it. A pretty young woman answered the door clad in skimpy bedroom wear. A tussled nest of red hair was piled on top of her head. Her sharp green eyes widened when she got her first look at Bolan, and her full red lips parted enough to offer a sort of mewing sound.

"Hi," Bolan said before pushing her back inside and closing the door behind him. "Are you the madam here or just one of the hired help?"

"Th-the what?" she stammered. "I don't know—"

"Don't be coy," Bolan warned. "My fight's not with you—it's with Mickey Gowan. Can you give him a message?"

The woman nodded quickly.

"Tell him Jeff Kellogg sends his regards. Can you remember that?"

"Yes…sure."

"Good. Now grab your friends and get out of here."

The woman turned immediately and rushed up the steps just as two more hardmen burst through a door on the opposite side of the room in one of the wings. Bolan crouched and tracked the arrivals with his pistol. The pair tried to find cover but stumbled over each other in their efforts to get out of the line of fire.

Bolan used the confusion to his advantage and dispatched the first with a single shot to the head. The other managed to get off two shots that buzzed past Bolan's ear, but the Executioner stood his ground and finished the guy with a shot to the chest.

Bolan continued through the house until he found the kitchen close to the rear. He could hear the scrambling of feet from activity on the second floor. He figured the four downed hardcases had constituted the entire security force for this place; he didn't think any would have been posted on the second floor. That's where business took place, and each of the girls probably had a panic button if things got out of hand. Typically, house rules kept security out of the business area unless they had a good reason to go into it.

Locating the gas line running from the stove to the wall, Bolan killed the gas flow at the valve, cut a deep furrow in the gas line with his knife and then opened the valve. That part finished, he went back through the kitchen and charged up the steps to the second floor. The ladies of the house were running in every direction, gathering whatever few possessions they could. Bolan shouted at them to step it up and get out of the building. Most, still in various modes of undress, muttered or hissed at him but he ignored them. Within another minute the entire place lay quiet and empty.

Bolan returned to the first floor, yanked two of the flash-bang grenades from his belt and armed them. He opened the door to the kitchen, rolled the grenades inside and then sprinted for the front door. He just cleared the porch when the natural-gas-fed explosion blew out the kitchen and the better part of the framing in that area. Bolan knew the failsafe valves would kick in, and the sheer distance of the house from the neighbors posed no real threat of damage to the surrounding structures. By the time the fire department arrived, however, the house would be consumed by flames.

Bolan didn't return to his vehicle, but instead commandeered a sedan that belonged to one of the thugs guarding the brothel. He stowed his weapons in the trunk save for the Beretta and then headed for his next target. He'd put his plan in motion; now he would wait and see how Gowan reacted.

BOLAN'S SECOND TARGET wouldn't prove as easy as the first. He watched through night-vision binoculars as eight armed men paired off to form four roving patrols intersecting the front and rear entrances to the building at one-minute intervals. That didn't give Bolan enough time to cross the nearly eight yards to the perimeter, cut through the fence line and cross the thirty or so additional yards before he reached either entrance. This would have to be a less subtle play, a luxury not afforded him at the first hardsite.

Bolan continued his watchful vigil for another twenty minutes before returning to his borrowed sedan and donning his war tools once more. This time, Bolan procured an HK53 from the trunk to accompany him in the assault. Heckler & Koch had designed this particular variant of the MP-5 to chamber 5.56 mm ammo, which made it more effective in area of coverage and stopping power. Like the FN-FNC, the HK53 had proved a formidable ally in the war on terror.

Bolan secured the trunk, got behind the wheel and started the engine. He checked his watch and then swung the nose and powered into a smooth acceleration. Bolan turned onto the access road that led to the storage yard, his wheels crunching on the gravel. The storage building allegedly contained special milling equipment and other supplies for the majority of timber operations in the area, but it also warehoused a weapons and money cache for Gowan's operations, never mind the drug lab that operated in a secret bunker beneath the building.

Bolan killed his lights as he drew closer to the storage-yard gates. He'd only get one shot at this, and he knew perfect timing would be the main factor in the mission's success. Bolan increased speed as he gained the curve. Dense cloud cover had recently given way to a full moon, the only thing to illuminate Bolan's charge. The Executioner gritted his teeth as the sedan ripped through the chain-link gates. He dropped the sedan into low gear as he powered brakes and accelerator in concert. He spun the vehicle in a 180-degree turn, and the rear end impacted the heavy front door of the building. The screech of metal on metal gave way to a clanging sound as the trunk of the car tore the door from its hinges.

Looking to his left, Bolan spotted a pair of sentries running for his position, their SMGs up and ready, muzzles winking. He pointed the HK53 out the window with his left hand and squeezed off a sustained burst, the muzzle of the weapon barely climbing in his sturdy grip. One of the sentries took a triburst of high-velocity slugs to the upper torso. He danced backward, jerked with each impact and hit the ground a moment later with the better part of his chest and stomach laid wide open. The second guard had the good sense to eat dirt in a moment of survival instinct, but Bolan tracked him. Several rounds ripped into the man's back and shattered his spine before a final burst to the top of his head finished him.

Bolan got clear of his vehicle and used it for cover from the approach of another pair of sentries from the right. They showed a little sooner than expected, but the Executioner was prepared. A short burst folded the first target in two as Bolan's 5.56 mm NATO rounds punched through the man's stomach and exposed his innards. The man dropped his weapon in shock, grabbing his entrails as he hit his knees and then fell prone to the pavement. His partner dropped and rolled expertly, narrowly avoiding Bolan's second and third bursts. The enemy sentry reached cover behind the concrete base of a light pole.

Bolan's gaze traversed upward and he swung the muzzle of his HK53 to follow. A few well-placed shots took out the light and rained sparks and glass on the man below. It also provided Bolan enough darkness to change positions and gain a better vantage point on his target. The soldier climbed through the back door of his vehicle, slid across the seat and came out the other side in a new firing position with his door for cover. He sighted on his now visible target and squeezed the trigger. The initial burst made contact and the impact knocked the guy off his feet.

It would take nearly a minute for the remaining quartet of sentries on the opposite side of the building to reach this point, which gave Bolan very little time to get inside and locate his target. This hit would require split-second timing and a bit of plain good luck.

Bolan moved inside the storage building and began his sweep. He checked the luminous dial of his watch again. He had no more than ninety seconds. Bolan passed a series of shelves stocked with machine parts for milling operations. Gowan had certainly gone to the trouble to make things look the part, although Bolan knew the place to be the false front that it was. He continued his search and soon found a section of wall that, under other circumstances, would have nicely concealed itself as the entrance to the underground drug lab. In this case, however, the half-dozen armed men standing guard on the wall belied its importance.

Bolan crouched as he liberated an M-67 fragmentation grenade from his load-bearing harness. He gave the sentry team another once-over before shaking his head and priming the grenade. Gowan's men were obviously committed, but they didn't appear to have the first clue on tactics. Clustered together, they only made Bolan's job easier. He yanked the pin, let the grenade cook off two seconds and then rolled it across the concrete floor in the direction of his target.

The sound of oblong metal rolling and scratching against the concrete drew the attention of the guards immediately. But in the dimness of the storage facility they didn't come to the realization death had just rolled to a stop against the boot toe of one among their ranks until a moment too late. The high explosive filled that moment with a concussion that separated limbs from the closest guards and knocked the rest off their feet. The thunderous blast of superheated gases released from the explosion threatened to deafen the Executioner, but he opened his mouth and covered his ears with his palms to avoid disorientation.

In the aftermath of the explosion Bolan was up and moving, the HK53 held at the ready, although no challengers remained standing. A couple of the guards were still alive but in no condition to offer resistance. Bolan examined the wall and spied a neat door-size seam in the wall. He quickly spotted a small groove to the right at about waist level and behind it he noted what felt like a latch. He pushed it into his fingers and the wall appeared to melt away as the door, heavy like that of a vault, swung inward.

Bolan advanced through the doorway and into a narrow corridor that made an abrupt turn and merged into a descending stairwell. Dim bulbs cast a greenish haze in the shadowy corridor.

The warrior descended the steps that emerged into a massive room. The acrid stench of methamphetamines processing stung

Bolan's nostrils. Several lab techs suited in protective gear turned
in his direction with looks of surprise. The man who appeared
to be the head guy, wearing a respirator and a lab coat, turned
toward the nearby wall to pull a lever, but Bolan beat him to the
punch. The Executioner snap-aimed the HK53 and triggered a
short volley that ripped through the man's arm.

As the echo of the subgun's reports died in the cavernous
room, Bolan said loudly, "Get out...*now!*"

There were no further arguments or attempts to call for help;
instead, all the occupants rushed past Bolan and up the stairs as
fast as their legs could carry them. Bolan waited until the echoes
of their departure died and then quickly primed the remaining
three M-67 grenades and tossed them onto the tables. He then
turned and dashed up the stairs as fast as his legs would carry him.

Bolan emerged on the first floor in time to meet the other four
sentries. They were surprised to see him but not nearly as much
as when he dived suddenly and rolled away from the wall
entrance. The explosions sounded a moment after Bolan went
prone, and for a few seconds the quartet of guards stood there,
puzzled. Then the compression from the explosive gases traversed up the steps and belched from the corridor like steam from
a pipe, and toxic gases heated by flame washed over the four-
some. The men staggered backward from the force of the blasts
as the heat scorched all of their body hair and in some points
seared the flesh from their bones. Two were killed instantly while
the other pair strutted like a pair of dancing torches. Bolan ended
their misery with well-placed mercy shots and then scrambled
to his feet and headed for the exit. It wouldn't be long before the
whole place went up.

The Executioner had scored another shot against Mickey
Gowan's crime empire and turned the tables on a potential traitor.
Now, one last target remained—the Bolan blitz continued.

IN THE VERY EARLY-MORNING hours following the assault on the
storage yard, Bolan returned to his rental sedan he'd left parked

near the brothel and headed to the club in Timber Vale. He hadn't even bothered to strip off his equipment.

The Executioner parked his vehicle in front of the club and dashed up the entrance steps. When he tried the door and found it locked, he aimed a swift kick six inches below the handle. The flimsy wooden door nearly came off its hinges, splintering in several places under the soldier's strength. Bolan pushed inside and found the place dark—a state that didn't necessarily translate as empty—but quickly located the back door. He opened it and heard sounds below of a party in full swing.

Time to crash it, Bolan thought. He headed down the steps that opened to a brightly lit room filled with people drinking, laughing and shouting to be heard over some sort of pop music blaring over unseen speakers. A night baseball game was playing on an HD big screen at the far end of the room. A massive board on another wall kept the tallies, and several manned phones were ringing incessantly. Nobody noticed Bolan until he whipped the Beretta into play and placed a 3-round burst through the television. By the time he put three more into the stereo deck, not only had everyone noticed him but he also had their undivided attention. The place had gone as quiet as a morgue.

Bolan cleared his throat. "Evening, folks. I hate to break up the party but you are now officially closed. Time for everyone to leave."

One of the guys in a tie and jacket standing near the bookmakers manning the phones stepped forward. "Who do you think you are?" he asked in a thick Irish accent.

"Me? Oh, just another do-gooder. I was sent by Jeff Kellogg to let all of you know this establishment is hereby closed, forthwith. Hence, I'd suggest you find some other place to do your gambling. Some other town, in fact, because this one's now off-limits to this kind of thing."

"What are you talking about?" another goon said. "I know Jeff Kellogg personally. He'd never roll over on Mickey."

Bingo.

"He would to save his own hide," Bolan said. "Now those of

you carrying, and I know exactly which three you are, toss your hardware on the floor."

The three enforcers Bolan had spotted almost immediately on reaching the stairwell landing did as ordered. He got them on the floor, and then ordered everyone else to leave. There were no arguments. The Executioner then gathered all the paper and liquor bottles he could find, piled them on the long desk of phones and lit the stack on fire. Then he ordered the trio of gunmen to strip to nothing but underwear and escorted them outside and across the street.

"You can wait here for the fire department," Bolan said.

"You're a fucking dead man," the leader said evenly. "Mickey will make sure of that."

"Yeah, sure," Bolan replied in a tone of pure mockery. "Gowan's empire is doomed. You can let him know that when you see him."

And with that, the Executioner walked up the street, climbed into his sedan and drove away. He checked his watch and realized he had only a few hours to sleep before his shift at the mill started. He'd operated on much less than that. The thought made Bolan smile.

He wouldn't want to be late for his first day on the job.

8

A couple of minutes after Bolan's departure from the motel, the local police arrived along with the sheriff and state trooper vehicles.

For the next four hours, Sandra Newbury spent every minute trying to convince law enforcement that the blabbering idiot she'd arrested was crazy, that she hadn't been with anyone else and that the suspect's claim that a big man with cold blue eyes had waved the muzzle of a pistol under his chin was absolute bunk. It probably wouldn't have taken that long for Newbury to get the authorities to cut her loose, especially seeing she'd acted in self-defense, but they were constantly interrupted by other disturbances. From what she gleaned in radio transmissions, those disturbances involved buildings going up in flames and reports of heavy gunfire.

Cripes, what was Cooper trying to do out there, start his own private war?

Well, she didn't give a damn anymore what he did as long he kept her out of it from that point on. Newbury had her own troubles to deal with, especially when they walked through the door in the form of Jeff Kellogg. Luckily, she managed to convince him that Cooper had actually held her hostage and she'd withheld the information from police until she was able to talk to Kellogg privately, since they were still officially working a classified federal case.

"I didn't know what else to do," she told him plaintively once they released her into Kellogg's custody as her official handler.

"You did the right thing," Kellogg assured her. "Just take it easy. Now tell me everything that happened again and give me all the details."

Newbury took a deep breath and then proceeded to hand Kellogg the biggest cockamamie story she could muster. She knew that half-truths were usually the most convincing, but she'd learned that when a man felt protective over a vulnerable woman, they would buy just about anything that woman handed him. In those cases, the more outrageous the story, the more believable it would be for the guy. Newbury related the tale exactly as she planned it—the four or so hours with the police had given her plenty of time to come up with a good one—and when she finished Kellogg didn't say anything for a very long time.

At last, he broke the silence. "So he admitted to killing one of Gowan's men. He actually *said* that he was the one who shot Billy Moran in cold blood."

She nodded. "That's exactly what he said."

"You know what doesn't make sense to me? Why this guy would bother to rescue you from a bunch of unknowns just to take you as a hostage."

"I told you already," Newbury said with exasperation. "He pegged me for an FBI agent, figured I had some insight into his operations."

Kellogg looked at her. "I've met this guy. I always figured him to be working with some other government agency. Covert ops or something."

Newbury shook her head. "I don't think so. He doesn't talk like one of us, and he sure as hell doesn't do things like one of us. Besides, do you really think the U.S. government would send a professional assassin to a peaceful lakeside community just to blow away some second-rate con artist with the Irish mob? They would leave it to us to get a guy like Moran legally."

Kellogg nodded. "Guess you're right."

"And there's another thing," Newbury said, casting her hook in now with the real bait. "I totally forgot. He said he thought you were working for Gowan."

Kellogg didn't say anything at first; he just looked at Newbury in surprise. Then he produced a chuckle that escalated into a guffaw, and Newbury decided to go along with it. She started laughing, too, although she kept his initial reaction gauged in the back of her mind. Damned if she and Cooper hadn't been right! Newbury had learned to read people long ago, one of the traits that made her good as an undercover agent.

Kellogg finally said, "What do *you* think?"

"I think it's bunk," she said. "Right?"

"Of course, Sandra," he replied easily.

Oh, so now they were on a first-name basis.

He slapped the steering wheel for emphasis and continued, "I think you're right about this guy not being from another agency. I thought for sure he was involved in black ops or something, but now I see he's just another cagey bastard with his own agenda. Otherwise he wouldn't have kept you locked up for so long. Did he hurt you?"

Newbury shook her head.

"By the way, how *did* you manage to escape?"

"He got into a firefight with those goons and when he heard the cops coming I guess he decided it wasn't worth taking me with him. So he cut me loose, told me not to tell anyone and then split."

"And knowing you were with the FBI, he probably figured you'd take the wrap for the shoot-out."

Newbury nodded. "And he was right. I just knew I couldn't tell the locals about him because it would compromise my cover."

"I don't think there's any doubt it's already compromised."

Actually, Newbury couldn't disagree with him on that count. Even if Cooper was one of the good guys, and he'd pretty much convinced her he was, he still knew she worked for the FBI and so did whoever he rescued her from that morning. Or had that been yesterday morning? Well, it didn't really matter because she had little time to sink her teeth into the angles and come up with some answers. One thing for sure, she didn't trust Kellogg anymore and she wasn't sure, outside of Cooper, who else she could trust at the FBI. She had to pursue this on her own.

"Well, if my cover's blown, then there's no point in going back."

"Right," Kellogg said. "I'll take you back to the office and you can file your reports. Oh, and one other thing. Did you happen to find out who it was that attacked you?"

"Nope. I'm not even sure why they attacked me."

"Meanwhile, I'm going to check it out what you've told me a bit more thoroughly."

"Looking for what?"

Kellogg shrugged. "Maybe I can find some connection between this Cooper and the guys who grabbed you."

They rode most of the remaining hours in silence, Newbury pondering the strangeness of it all and Kellogg thinking about who the hell knew what. Newbury felt relieved when they finally pulled up to FBI headquarters. She got out and noticed Kellogg hadn't moved. She stopped, tapped on the window and he rolled it down.

"You're not coming in?" she inquired.

"No," he said. "I have a couple places to go. And don't worry about doing all the paperwork right now. Just file a brief tonight and then get some rest. We'll do a more detailed report after that."

She nodded and he drove off, leaving her on the sidewalk, its surface still glistening with puddles left by the recent rainfall. Newbury turned and ascended the steps into the building. She didn't plan to file a report. In fact, she didn't plan to do anything about this right now. Kellogg had become her number-one case for the moment; she was convinced the guy was into something dirty.

Newbury went straight to the garage floor and checked out a vehicle from the motor pool. After she got a change of clothes from her temporary-duty-assigned quarters downtown, she'd head to Kellogg's place and sit on him until he made his next move. She'd have to be damned careful, to be sure, as Kellogg was nobody's fool and probably quite able to pick out a tail without too much trouble. It would take all of her skill this time around, but she felt it was worth it. One way or another, if Jeff Kellogg was into something dirty, Newbury meant to bring him down for the count.

As soon as Kellogg dropped off Newbury at headquarters, he dialed in the personal number for Sully Sullivan.

Sully's voice answered on the fifth ring. "It's six a.m.! What the hell do you want, yer yonker?"

"We need to meet. Right away."

Some of the edge left Sully's voice, although Kellogg could tell the man was irritated at being awoken. Tough. This was important, and Kellogg didn't mean for any time to go to waste. It didn't make a damned bit of difference to him if this Cooper blew up every goddamned business in Gowan's backyard—he didn't have any money invested in Gowan's interests—but he didn't want them able to say he knew about Cooper's activities and didn't warn them.

"Meet me at the usual place. An hour," Sully replied, and then Kellogg heard a click.

Kellogg looked at the phone a moment before closing the voice piece and tossing the phone on the seat next to him with a sigh of disgust. He didn't like the direction of this thing at all, and what Newbury had revealed to him only complicated things. How the hell did he get himself into this kind of shit anyway? All he originally looked to do was make a few extra bucks so he had a decent retirement to look forward to. Now he had pricks like Gowan and Jeter who treated him like little more than an errand boy.

And if things were about to heat up, he didn't want to be anywhere near it. Kellogg considered his options. Although he hated to admit it, he stood a hell of a lot better chance maintaining his alliances with Jeter than he did by keeping an association with Mickey Gowan. Jeter had wealth, power and influence; he stood as a liked and respected member of the community, especially among many of the power brokers in Washington, D.C. Such a man could make or break the career of a guy like Kellogg.

His decision made, Kellogg dialed Jeter's number but reached his voice mail. He left a message that he had a meeting and, as

soon as it was over, he would bring critical information to the
table that would seal their deal against Gowan, Cooper and the
rest of the crew in Timber Vale. Before the sun set that day, Kellogg
figured there would be a lot of blood spilled.

Thankfully, none of it would be his.

ONCE SHE GOT A SHOWER and change of clothes, Sandra
Newbury proceeded directly to Jeff Kellogg's condominium.
She drove once through the parking lot of the complex and didn't
see his car, so she parked in a spot marked for guests and proceeded to his unit. The door had one of those standard self-
locking handles, but with a lock-pick set from her purse Newbury
had the door open in under two minutes.

Newbury closed the door and studied the darkened interior for
a minute, letting her eyes adjust. Narrow bands of morning light
filtered through drawn curtains and shades. It seemed strange to
Newbury, as she advanced farther into the condominium, that
Kellogg covered every window. She lightly flicked a nearby
blind, and a cloud of dust danced upward into the stream of
sunlight. Kellogg obviously had his windows covered all the
time—seemed like an act of paranoia more than security.

What are you hiding, Kellogg? she asked herself.

Though it was unlikely an agent with Kellogg's savvy would
leave incriminating evidence lying around his house, she thought
maybe she could pick up a clue here or there. Newbury produced
a penlight and began to search drawers. She rifled through papers
but found little more than bills, tax returns and the occasional
porn magazine—nothing she wouldn't have expected in a bach-
elor pad. She then checked less obvious places looking for
anything, a safe or hidden compartment behind pictures or a
medicine cabinet, a false bottom to a kitchen drawer, but she
came up with nothing.

Finally, she turned her attention to the computer in the spare
room of the condo that Kellogg used as his office. To her surprise,
she found not only was the computer powered up but Kellogg

had left himself logged on. Well, didn't that beat all? At least she wouldn't have to try cracking any passwords. She quickly surfed through his Internet history, found nothing of interest and then moved on. She checked recently run programs and discovered some banking software. A few minutes later she was looking into his checking account. There were no obvious discrepancies, so she moved on to a link labeled Retirement Account. She clicked it, and the next thing to pop up was an investment portfolio with a firm based out of the Cayman Islands, the current distributions totaled more than a million dollars. No matter how wise his investments, Newbury knew there was no way in hell Kellogg could have that kind of money, even through inheritance. Her suspicion was confirmed when she dug deeper and found the regular wire deposits from an untraceable account out of Switzerland to the account of a company called KO Holdings. The amounts varied from ten to twenty-five thousand U.S. dollars.

While this told Newbury everything she needed to know about Kellogg's illicit activities, it wasn't any kind of real proof. The accounts could belong to anyone, and there wasn't any way to actually tie Kellogg to KO Holdings or to the investment firm that had been brokering the monies for him. It would take a lot more than that to bring down a senior agent in the FBI.

Newbury removed a thumb drive from her pocket, copied the financial files to it and then closed the programs and left things just as she'd found them. She exited the room, headed for the front door, but the sudden jangle of keys on the other side froze her in her tracks. Newbury's heartbeat quickened and a lump formed in her throat. She looked furiously for a place to hide, but nothing immediately presented itself. At the sound of the key in the door she whirled and rushed back to the makeshift office. She looked in the spare closet—it was empty so he'd have no reason to open it—and crouched. She performed an exercise she learned in aerobics to slow her breathing.

She remained still as he rustled about in the desk drawers then tapped his fingers across the computer keyboard. The minutes ticked by and her feet began to numb…then she heard him walk out.

She waited nearly a full minute before finally standing. The feeling returned to her calves in a warm flood. She shuddered against the thousands of little pinpricks in the soles of her feet as blood rushed to them. Damn it, what the hell was he doing? She put her ear to the door but try as she might, she couldn't hear anything.

When she caught the sound of the front door slamming, she waited for thirty seconds before venturing from the closet and into an empty living room. This time, she couldn't afford to lose Kellogg. She rushed out the door, down the walkway amid the buildings and dashed for her car. She climbed behind the wheel and looked down both ends of the street until the outline of Kellogg's cobalt-blue government sedan caught her eye. She started her car and set a pursuit course that would allow her to follow safely but avoid detection.

While she hated to admit it, Newbury realized everything hinged upon her discovering who paid Kellogg's bills, although she already had a pretty good idea who that was. She was off to a good start but she would need a lot more proof of his collusion with the bad guys before she could run it upstairs. This might just be her one opportunity to do it.

And Sandra Newbury had no intention of letting it slip through her fingers.

9

6:00 a.m. came early to Mack Bolan, who presently operated on a couple hours of sleep. He'd secured a new hotel room, in a neighboring town to act as his temporary base of operations, confident the local law enforcement would be less likely to look for him there. They probably had the vaguest of general descriptions. Once secured, he'd placed a call to Johnny, who hacked into the Jackson County sheriff's records to find that they had released Sandra Newbury into Kellogg's custody. Obviously, she had managed to provide a decent cover story, but it wouldn't take long for the locals to put it all together and realize his various activities in the area were related.

When Bolan showed for work as scheduled, they put him on the line immediately in his position as chaser. The job proved tough and hazardous but Bolan took to it like a fish to water, thanks to his good physical conditioning. They stopped at midmorning for a ten-minute break where he made small talk with the other chaser on the line. They got back into the swing of things and continued until the eleven-o'clock lunch whistle.

At lunch, Bolan went to MacDermott's office, but Sally advised that he'd stepped out. She didn't know where he was or even when he'd be back, but he had left a message for Bolan. She handed him an envelope. Bolan thanked her politely but waited until he could be alone to open the envelope. Inside he found a thousand-dollar bill and a note: Coop, here's a little something for your trouble at Backcut. Meet me there after your shift. Mac.

Bolan nodded, pocketed the Grover Cleveland and then tossed

the note into an open-fire stove used to burn off wood shavings and simultaneously to power steam-driven tools. He repressed a smile at the thought he'd won over MacDermott so quickly. Bolan was either walking into a trap or he really did have the guy's confidence; in any case, this would give him a full inside view to what was going on. Bolan figured MacDermott had to be getting pretty desperate at this stage of the game. He couldn't be entirely sure, but Bolan sensed MacDermott didn't have quite as large a following as Gowan. He hadn't proved himself yet, and most people would place a bet on the surest horse.

Time will tell, the Executioner thought as he bought a hot dog and drink off the food truck and found a place to eat in silence. Once he finished his lunch, he tried calling Newbury on her cell phone, but her voice mail picked up immediately. She had either turned the phone off or she was out of range. They needed to talk soon, though, discuss what she discovered about Kellogg. Word of Bolan's activities the previous night was also spreading like wildfire, and he heard quite a bit of it through the remainder of his shift. Some postulated a gang war among some of Mickey Gowan's goons while others figured it for a crime spree by out-of-towners. Any explanation suited the Executioner as long as his name didn't come into it.

As soon as Bolan finished his shift he got in his car and headed for Backcut. He spotted the tail almost immediately but decided not to do anything about it until they made some sort of aggressive move. A quick look at the vehicle told him it couldn't be the police, which would have surprised him anyway as he didn't think they would have his description on the airwaves so soon. Maybe it was more of Kellogg's goons or the ELF, maybe even someone MacDermott had put on his tail to see if Bolan was behaving himself. He'd have to keep his eyes open—the numbers were ticking down and the Executioner was running out of time.

BOLAN DECIDED THAT reconnoitering the area around Backcut would draw too much suspicion from his tail so he opted to drive straight to the bar for his meeting. He reached into the console and clipped the Beretta into shoulder leather beneath his flannel shirt jacket before climbing from his vehicle and moving inside. He went straight to the bartender and asked for MacDermott; the bartender jerked a thumb to a heavy wooden door in the back and Bolan nodded his thanks.

A minute later, he stood inside a cramped room with an oversize table. Half the chairs ranged around it were occupied by men Bolan didn't recognize save for Fagan MacDermott and his number-one bootlicker, Flannery. He figured the other guys either had ties to the mill, the union or the local businesses in town that were paying on Gowan's loans.

"Coop, me boy!" MacDermott called, then gestured toward a chair. "Grab a seat."

Bolan did as requested and greeted the other men with a nod. MacDermott made more formal introductions, and Bolan filed each name away for future reference.

"Everyone's here, so let's get this show on the road," Mac-Dermott said. "You all know why I called this meeting. I've been talking with some of my boys who are working angles down by Gowan, and they tell me now's the time to act. We won't get another chance like this."

"Chance like this?" piped in Ed Kofahl, owner of the only tailor shop in town. "Mickey Gowan's got his fingers into everything, Mac, see? There ain't no way he's going to give up the mill without a fight."

"Eddie's right," Flannery said. "The count between us and Gowan right now is at least two-to-one, maybe even three-to-one."

"That don't make a shite," MacDermott replied. "We got something Gowan ain't got…we got the workers on our side. You see, I've been watching everything that's going on. And I've always taken care of all of us, haven't I?"

The group nodded.

MacDermott continued, "We don't need no more of Gowan's money with the huge vigorish on top of it. The guy's a weasel.

And I found out just how much a weasel when I hired old Coop here. You see, Cooper's ex-military and an expert with explosives. And he's got a little side job here working for some folks that ain't too happy with Mickey right now. Tell 'em about it, Coop." He thumbed in Bolan's direction and told the others, "Listen to this."

"The money you took doesn't belong to Mickey Gowan," Bolan said.

"Eh?" said a guy they called Spense. "What do you mean it ain't Mickey's money?"

"Just like I said. It isn't his. It belongs to the people I work for. Powerful people. And they think it's *you,* the business owners and workers in Timber Vale, who have stolen it from them."

"That's bullshit!" Flannery said. He jumped to his feet and pointed at Bolan. "We didn't steal nothing from nobody!"

"Easy," MacDermott said. "Sit your keester down and let Coop finish."

Flannery complied and Bolan continued, "I've managed to convince the people who hired me that Gowan's managed to pull the wool over your eyes and that the people here are good people, that Mickey Gowan's taken advantage of that goodness."

"Excellent," Spense replied.

"But," Bolan continued, "this is still their money and business is business. They want it back and they don't care how they get it."

"So what's the bottom line?" Kofahl asked.

"Just like Mac's telling you. We need to take the fight to Mickey Gowan, and we need to do it now before my friends change their minds."

"And how do we do that?"

"I have sources who tell me there's a Fed named Jeff Kellogg who's on Gowan's payroll. But Kellogg's started getting a bit greedy and started to kick down some doors in this area. He's already hit several of Gowan's businesses in town and he's made a lot of noise about it. What I'm afraid will happen is he hits one of your businesses next. Some of his people already tried to manhandle Louise."

"From Lamplighter?" Spense asked. He expressed incredulity to MacDermott.

The union boss nodded. "Yeah and I confirmed it actually happened. I guess Coop here arrived in the nick of time to keep something real bad from happening."

"Well, I sure as hell ain't going to have nobody coming into my business and manhandling my people. Ain't no way in hell that's going to happen."

"It'll happen if we don't act now," Bolan said. "You wanted the bottom line? I'll give it to you. Timber Vale needs to stick up for itself and decide right now who's running this show. Is it the citizens of the town or Mickey Gowan? If it's you folks, then you need to do the right thing."

"Yeah, sure," Kofahl said, "but violence never solves nothing. I mean most of these folks are just good people, like you say. We can't fight no war."

"Well, then Gowan's going to walk all over you. And you're going to get blamed for the money he allegedly lost, and then there isn't a thing I can do to help you." Bolan threw up his hands for emphasis. "Understand, it isn't any skin off my nose. I get paid either way. But I'm a businessman just like you, and I don't think a guy like Mickey Gowan's good for business. He's the kind of guy that uses people. It's up to you to decide whether you're going to let him continue using you or do something about it."

"What do you have in mind?" Spense asked.

Bolan shook his head. "Mac here already has a plan. There isn't much I can do for that."

"I can fill in Coop on his assignment later," MacDermott interjected. "For now, we should concentrate on the big game plan. We've staged the mill workers strike to start first thing tomorrow morning. Nobody's going to show at work. After that, I'll make the call to Mickey and let him know. I'm sure he'll want to send up some of his boys at that point."

"And that's when we'll hit them!" Flannery smacked a fist into his open palm.

"Now don't go getting a hard-on so quick," MacDermott warned.

"Right," Bolan added. "I won't be so anxious to die if I were you."

"Well, you ain't me," Flannery countered. "And what makes you think it's me that's going to die? I got me an entire crew just waiting—"

"That'll do!" MacDermott cut in.

His reaction surprised Bolan a little. The tone of voice and quickness to interrupt made it almost seem as if MacDermott was trying to stop Flannery from saying too much. That made him wonder if MacDermott didn't trust Bolan or he doubted one of the others at the table. It especially made him curious to know he'd get his assignment in private, particularly given MacDermott's reference to his expertise in explosives. Just what exactly did the guy have in mind?

"Now, once Gowan's people get here we'll go ahead and spring our little surprise. That should give me enough to bargain with, at least a position to bring to the bargaining table. Then once we have Timber Vale in control, we'll make the payoff to Cooper's people and all will be well."

"And just exactly how much do we owe?" Kofahl asked, looking at Cooper expectantly.

"I wasn't told," Bolan replied quickly, "but I'm sure they would accept thirty-five percent as a fair settlement."

"Thirty-five per—?" Kofahl stopped in midsentence and jerked his thumb at Bolan. "Where the hell did you get this guy? He's out of his friggin' mind, Mac!"

MacDermott waved his hand in a gesture of placation. "Let's not jump to any conclusions right now, okay? He just said he wasn't told. I'm sure he's estimating high."

"I sure the hell hope so," Spense said.

Bolan decided to add to the damage control, solidify his good position with MacDermott some. "Like I said before, guys, my people are fair. They just want what they got coming to them.

They aren't looking to take what's not theirs. But they are going to get what belongs to them one way or another. The only question that remains is to what lengths they'll go to get it. They're not interested in a bloodbath—such things attract attention."

"Look," Spense said, "let's just cut the shit. Who are we really talking about here?"

Bolan sighed. "We're talking about people capable of bringing down two fighter jets and disappearing before anyone knows what really happened."

Bolan knew his declaration was a gamble, but he didn't have any other cards to deal. He had little doubt the Earth Liberation Front was behind the attacks on the military aircraft at Kingsley Airfield, and he knew the incident had captured national news attention. For all he knew, they were ready to lash out against Gowan and his holdings, and he didn't want innocents caught up in a bloody war between terrorists and criminals. No matter what MacDermott might think, they were hardly prepared to deal with something like that—it didn't matter how many hard cases Flannery had managed to round up. Both of those entities would be able to call upon nothing short of a private army.

"You may have a chance to settle things peacefully with Mickey Gowan," Bolan continued now that he had their attention, "but don't think for a second you can stand up to the people who hired me. They'll cut this town to ribbons."

"So what are you suggesting?" Spense asked.

"Take out Gowan's operation and give them their money back before they stop playing nice guy."

"I'd have to say he's right, Mac," another business owner said, speaking for the first time. "There's no question that they're already kicking down doors all over town. They got the cathouse over in the nice part of town, and O'Halloran's went up in smoke early this morning. We all know they were running a numbers racket in the basement, and all that cash was going into Mickey's pocket."

"And that's the tip of the iceberg," Bolan concluded. He locked eyes with MacDermott. "It'll only get worse from here."

"Okay, okay," MacDermott replied. "So you guys got me thinking a little harder about this. It still doesn't make any difference so far as I'm concerned. We'll follow our plan and just hope to hell Mickey decides it's better for him to walk away peacefully than try to fight an entire town."

"Sounds like he'll have enough to worry about already when he finds out what's happening to his places of business," Flannery offered.

"Yeah," MacDermott mumbled. "Let's just hope the timing of our own thing doesn't seem too convenient for what's happening. Otherwise, it could have a reverse effect."

Bolan thought about responding to that but at the last minute chose to keep his mouth shut. He'd already considered those angles. Mickey Gowan was smart enough to know that Kellogg wasn't behind those hits. The crime boss would see right through the facade as soon as someone gave him Bolan's description. The only reason he'd even bothered to drop Kellogg's name was to send a message to both men that he knew of their association. That would buy them some additional trouble once word got around Gowan had a federal agent on his payroll. It might also help keep Kellogg at bay and lessen the risks to Newbury.

This staged strike had turned out to be nothing more than luck of the draw. Bolan could convince them to stand up for themselves against Gowan, which would cause the citizens to rally behind one another. Bolan could then turn his attention to the ELF, the ones he considered to be a much bigger threat. Taking Gowan out of business would be an added bonus—he could accomplish two missions simultaneously.

After a few details the meeting broke up. Bolan remained behind to talk with MacDermott. He couldn't say it bothered him when MacDermott ordered Flannery to take a hike. The guy was volatile; he didn't trust him. He decided to tell MacDermott as much.

"Eh, don't worry about Chep. He'll do what he's told. Which brings me to you." MacDermott took a long pull from his fifth mug of beer and smacked his lips. He wiped away foam with the back of his hand and said, "I need you tell me I can trust you."

Bolan shook his head but replied, "Okay. You can trust me, Mac."

"Good enough for me," MacDermott said. He toasted Bolan and took another long swig, then continued, "I take it you know your way around town pretty well."

"I can get by."

"Fine." He gave him an address. "I want you to go there and pick up two packages from a guy. He's already been paid so you don't have to worry about carrying no cash on you. Just pick up the packages and bring them to the mill tonight."

"Mind if I ask what's in them?"

MacDermott emitted a closemouthed laugh around a cigarette he was lighting. "I'd be surprised if you didn't. Let's just say they're some party favors I'll need you to light off for me if Mickey decides a hostile takeover would be easier."

"Sounds like you're expecting trouble."

"Only if that greedy Mick comes looking for it," MacDermott replied.

10

Jeff Kellogg's request for a meeting had started as mere annoyance to Struthers Sullivan, but after he heard what the guy had to tell him, the situation became critical.

Sully had served Mickey Gowan faithfully for many years, but Gowan had a bad habit of not listening when Sully offered advice, which especially angered Sully since he never offered his counsel unbidden. Entering into any kind of partnership with Kellogg had gone against Sully's better judgment. Still, Gowan had chosen not to listen to him, and now Sully sensed that could cost them. A lot.

"In what way?" Gowan asked at their private table in his favorite country club. After lunch, Gowan had booked his afternoon for eighteen holes of golf.

"I think he's working undercover."

"For the Feds?"

Sully shook his head. "No, for Percy Jeter's crew."

Mickey Gowan studied Sully's face for a long moment and then burst into laughter with a wave of his hand. "Bah! That yonker couldn't keep up with someone like Jeter. And I can't see him putting a weasel like Kellogg on the payroll. He thinks too much of himself for that."

"I wouldn't be too sure, boss," Sully replied in an even tone of voice. "I told you there was something about that guy. I didn't trust him from the beginning, and I still don't."

"You've always had it in for him, Sully."

"And I think I have a good reason. You know this Cooper character you asked me to take care of? The guy's as slippery as a fish, Mickey. He's never in one place long enough for me to take him out, not to mention he's getting a whole lot of people riled up with his shenanigans up in Timber Vale."

"What shenanigans?" Gowan said, turning his full attention to Sully from the plate of cabbage, sausage and boiled potatoes just set in front of him.

"He's already hit three of our places and tried to blame Kellogg for it. Like we ain't gonna know it wasn't Kellogg, or something."

"If it's like you say, Sully, Cooper is the least of our problems." Gowan shoved in a first bite and around a mouthful asked, "You tailing him?"

"Who?"

"Kellogg."

"Yeah, I've got a couple of the boys on him. They called in once to report he'd gone back to his house and that's about all they could say. I haven't heard from them since."

"Okay, so what you do you think this yonker's going to do?"

Sully didn't want to admit he really hadn't thought of that before now. He answered, "I'm not sure. That's why I put a tail on him."

Gowan took a swig of beer and said, "All right, then, Sully. You keep an eye on him. And as to this Cooper, I can't have him going around and blowing up and setting fire to my businesses, see. You got to put this son of a bitch down, and do it quick. Ya hearing me? We can't have this."

"I hear you, boss."

"All right, I guess that's it for now."

Sully got up and left the table. There wasn't anything more he could do here talking to Gowan; he had plenty of other things to take care of, starting with finding Cooper and putting an end to his activities.

As soon as Sully was in his car headed for Timber Vale, he called ahead to let his lieutenants know of his impending arrival. As Gowan had ordered Cooper eliminated, Sully would have to attend the matter personally. Kellogg's activities had him concerned, but he'd have to rely on his men to keep him apprised of the Fed's movements and not worry too much. Kellogg might not be planning to do anything stupid at all, although Sully doubted it. Before the evening was through he'd probably have to deal with *two* problems.

It took three hours to negotiate the winding roads through Siskiyou Pass, and the late-afternoon sun edged the mountaintops by the time he pulled into Timber Vale. He drove straight to the main downtown office complex. Part of a single-story strip mall, the sign out front advertised the office as an insurance agency.

Sully entered the office and received a polite greeting from the receptionist at the front desk. He waved casually at her with a smile before proceeding to the glass enclosure of a single office in the rear, the supposed domain of the general manager, Artus Parrish. Actually, Parrish was Sully's lieutenant in charge of collections. The two men shook hands warmly and then Sully grabbed a seat.

"So, tell me what's going on," Sully said. "And I want details, Arty."

Parrish described the attacks on Mickey Gowan's various enterprises: the brothel, the warehouse and the basement casino. He told stories that sounded almost preposterous to Sully, who merely listened and made no comment until he got the entire story. After Parrish finished his narrative, Sully sat in brooding contemplation for some minutes.

"Explosives, you say," Sully repeated. "Grenades maybe and some automatic rifles, too?"

Parrish nodded. "Yeah, Sully, I'm telling you this yonker came out of nowhere like he was some kind of commando or something. The boys said he was dressed all in black, head-to-toe black, they said."

"What else?"

"What the shite you mean, like besides he looked and acted like a demon from hell?"

Sully waved a hand and grumbled, "Don't be dramatic. You got to stay cool, you understand, Arty? If the guys see you getting all uptight, they're going to get the same way."

"Okay, all right, Sully," Parrish replied. "Have it your way."

"Now, tell me about this other thing."

"What other thing?"

"You know, the thing with Fagan. Word came to me he's been mouthing off around town, talking down about Mickey and such. What's the story with that?"

Parrish shrugged. "Don't be bothered about Mac. He's just spouting off the usual stuff, about how he's got the control on everything. Everybody knows Mad Mac's just full of hot air. He's a little fish in a big pond."

"Yeah, well, don't tell me to not be bothered by it, Arty, because this guy's talking just a little too much. Somebody needs to close his mouth."

"Fine, Sully, fine," Parrish said in surrender. "I'll take care of it. Meanwhile, you should probably be more worried about this Cooper. He's a real problem, that one. He's going to ruin everything if you don't stop him."

"Oh, I'll stop him," Sully replied. "Just find out where he is."

THE FIRST THING Sandra Newbury noticed was that she was following the follower. At first she thought it was just stress, but she realized she had seen that forest-green sports car one too many times to consider it mere coincidence. Especially given that Kellogg's little trip was turning out to be more than a mere jaunt. As they continued out of California and into Siskiyou she noticed less and less traffic.

Soon they were on a two-lane, winding road with a series of switchbacks that took them to a higher altitude. At one point they had to wait almost two hours while road crews cleared a massive chunk of ice and snow that had fallen from the cliff face. As they climbed it got darker and darker. Everywhere Kellogg stopped, Newbury had to just sit and wait, watching the two men who were obviously watching Kellogg. Both were big men dressed in suits and overcoats. They neither looked nor carried themselves like Feds, so Newbury figured they were

Mickey Gowan's men. Probably ordered to keep tabs on Kellogg's movements.

As Kellogg and his tail pulled into a service station—advertised as the last facility available until the bottom of the mountain pass a good fifty miles the other side of the summit—Newbury drove past the station slowly and parked an eighth of a mile up the highway at an overlook. She picked her way along the slippery, treacherous trail of dry and overgrown brush bordering the roadway until she reached the station. She took a position in the tree line and studied the parking lot. One of the pair in the sports car pumped gas while the other used a pay phone mounted to the exterior of the station. Newbury couldn't be certain, but it looked like the two men were exchanging glances. Five minutes passed, then another five minutes, but Kellogg didn't reappear outside.

What the hell was the guy doing in there?

Newbury kept looking at her watch and still nobody appeared. Only one vehicle left the station during the time, a black van with windows too dark to see inside. Newbury continued her vigil for a few more minutes and then headed back to her car. She now felt chilled to the bone. The tennis shoes she had worn were hardly adequate to protect her feet from the snowy-wet ground, and her teeth chattered by the time she returned to her vehicle. She started the engine and cranked the heater, then considered her options.

She only had to think a minute and then considered the van again. Damn! Kellogg wasn't still inside that store. He'd probably gone out the back and climbed into that minivan! Newbury dropped the gearshift into drive and tromped the accelerator. The wheels spun up ice and gravel as she tore from the promontory parking area and fishtailed up the hill. She looked at her watch, figured maybe the vehicle would be five or six minutes ahead of her. With any luck, she'd be able to catch it.

She had to hand it to Kellogg; he'd pulled off a very clever ruse. Nearly pulled it off, that was. Newbury's heart beat hard and steadily in her chest. If she'd lost him it would prove damned difficult to pick up the trail again. Whoever he'd come to meet here apparently intended to keep that meeting a secret, and damned if she let them get away with it. Cooper was counting on her to gather intelligence on Kellogg's activities, as was the FBI, and she couldn't let them down—and she sure as hell couldn't let herself down by losing her quarry after coming so far.

The appearance of taillights rounding the curve ahead brought her back into focus. As she rounded the curve, the briefest flash of light shone in her rearview mirror and then disappeared. She kept her eyes to the road, checking every now and then, but didn't see anything. She accelerated just a little more, careful not to overextend the speed at which she could respond to all the twists and turns in the road.

An abrupt, wrenching force from behind caused her knees to strike the dash just below the steering column. She cried out in pain, but the seat belt locked and kept her body from slamming into the steering wheel. As the shock passed, she realized something had struck her from the rear. She looked into her rearview mirror and bright lights practically blinded her. She looked at the winding road ahead, intent on keeping her sedan under control, but the driver rear-ended her again and she began to fishtail. Newbury struggled with the steering wheel, a painful venture as she had sprained her wrist against it on the second impact. She pumped her brakes to no avail, and it took every ounce of will just to keep the vehicle from spinning out of control and straight off the mountainside.

The screech of metal on metal resounded in her ears as sparks danced up along the driver's window. She'd somehow struck a guardrail and realized her car was traveling backward. Newbury pumped the brakes, which seemed to help a bit, but the car was still traveling too fast. In a last-ditch effort, she disengaged her seat belt, jerked the wheel in the opposite direction and then opened the door. She leaped from the car, tucking her chin to her chest as her body hit the hard and cold ground, and rolled to her feet. Her car struck a tree on the shoulder and spun to a halt. The van, which had rushed past her just prior to the accident, performed a U-turn and rocketed toward her.

Newbury drew her pistol and prepared to defend what little hope for life remained.

11

"I've got a real sweet deal for you," Fagan MacDermott told the Executioner.

After completing their meeting, MacDermott took Bolan back to the mill. Everyone had gone for the day. The place was dark, and long shadows were cast throughout the interior by a few security lamps. The machines were silent, the yarding line devoid of all movement. Only the tap-tap of the cooling metal of the stoves bore any witness humans had ever occupied the place. It seemed almost foreboding in this state, but Bolan considered this an opportunity.

MacDermott took him to a pair of heavy sliding doors that were chained and padlocked. Bolan had noticed this area during the day, but he never got too close as he didn't want anyone seeing him sniffing around. He'd planned to come back at night to do a soft probe, but now MacDermott planned to make it easy for him. The big Irishman unlocked the doors, then slid them aside and gestured for Bolan to enter. He stepped over the threshold and MacDermott followed, shutting the door behind them before engaging a light switch. Overhead recessed lights bathed the area in a warm, red glow. The room was about half the width of the rest of the factory, long and narrow with a low ceiling. In the red tint of the lighting it seemed to stretch on forever, although it really wasn't that large. Crates were pushed to both sides of the walls and surrounded a bare wood table in the center.

The sharp, fruity scent of nitro-based solvents, gun oil and silicone rags permeated Bolan's sense of smell and left no doubt he stood amid a large weapons cache. MacDermott gestured to one of the nearby crates, square and marked with the warnings and hazardous-materials placard identifying ordnance. He slid a key from his pocket, opened the padlocked sealing the box and flipped the lid. Inside lay quarter-pound rectangular sticks of C-4 plastique.

"Impressive, eh?" MacDermott said.

Bolan nodded.

"It's not military-grade, of course, but it'll do the trick."

"And what exactly did you have in mind for this stuff?" Bolan asked. He gestured around the room and said, "It looks like you got enough here to supply a small army."

"We do," MacDermott said and he closed the lid. "But this stuff is what will change Mickey's mind in a hurry. Make him think twice about refusing our offer, eh?"

"Far be it for me to spoil the fun. But have you thought this through carefully?"

MacDermott could have taken offense, but Bolan didn't register any in his expression. That worried him as the guy had seemed pretty emotional about the whole thing before but now he seemed cool, collected. He seemed more than capable of taking charge of the entire operation and seeing it through until the very end, and a guy who didn't let his emotions get the better of him would be more difficult to control; it wouldn't prove as easy to manipulate MacDermott as Bolan first believed.

"What do you mean, asking if I thought this through? Of course I thought it through." MacDermott pivoted and began to pace as spoke, waving his arms. "You said it yourself, Coop. Mickey's not going to give up without a fight. He's been sticking it to the people of this town for a long time, making a lot of money off their backs. I like these folks, and I'm tired of seeing them get the shaft by guys like Gowan. It's time we fight back."

"You're talking about bringing war to this town," Bolan said. "How's that going to help people, Mac?"

MacDermott whirled, the red in his face visible even in the ruby hue cast by the lighting. "Because we don't have to run and hide anymore, that's how! You don't know what it's like, Coop. You've been here just a couple of days. But a lot of us have been here for many a year, and we're tired of killing ourselves for pennies while Gowan reaps all the profits. And you want to know what's more? The guy's obviously been doing nothing to stick out his own neck for these folks. He hasn't even bothered to loan them his own money to invest in businesses, take a risk and all. Naw! Instead he's using the money of others, of some really bad people."

"Fine," Bolan replied. "You're upset the guy's been sticking it to innocent people. Nobody understands that better than I do. Believe me. But you're talking about a lot of bloodshed for something you may not be able to win."

"We *can* win it with the right leadership. My kind of leadership. I ain't nothing great, mind you, Coop, but I'm all these people have." He offered a grin Bolan found hard to resist.

Bolan nodded. At first he'd considered Fagan MacDermott nothing more than just another thug looking to gain power and wealth at the expense of others, but now he realized MacDermott wasn't really one of the bad guys. And it seemed he'd rallied for a cause to which the Executioner had no trouble relating—the suppression of those who would try to exploit the weak and prey on the innocent.

"So what is it you want me to do?" Bolan asked.

"Well, that's the good thing. You see, Chep's bringing his boys here in a little while to get all of this shite outta here. I want you to keep an eye on things, make sure it doesn't go wrong. About an hour ago, I arranged for my message to be sent to Mickey. I'm sure he's got it by now, which means before dawn he'll have his crew up here at the mill to make sure nothing happens to it. If he sends them here, and I mean *only* if he sends them, I want you to level this place. You think you can do that for me, Coop? Eh?"

Bolan nodded. "Yeah, I can do that."

"Great!" MacDermott clapped his hands and rubbed them vigorously. "I knew I could count on you. Now, let's go have a drink and seal up this deal."

"Actually, I've got to make some phone calls."

"Nonsense," MacDermott with a wave as they walked out of the room. "You got plenty of time to do that later."

MacDermott sealed the door, and the two walked out of the mill and into the chilly air of sunset. A steady wind had picked up, making the evening more cold and damp than it had seemed when they went inside. Bolan got behind the wheel of his sedan as MacDermott climbed into his truck. The Executioner considered eluding the guy but thought better of it. Probably not the best time to cut and run when he'd just built the man's trust. Besides, he couldn't walk on the town now that a war might break out between Gowan's army of hard guys and the entourage of common laborers MacDermott and Flannery had formed. The latter would be no match against trained killers; even if they had the superior numbers Bolan figured they were outclassed.

Bolan followed MacDermott's truck out of the lot and as they rounded the bend leading from the mill, the Executioner had to stand on his brakes. A pair of black SUVs blocked the road along with a dozen armed men, some inside the vehicles and others under covered firing positions. Bolan popped the trunk and rolled out on the passenger's side, using the door for cover as he dashed for the trunk in a crouched run. He made it halfway before the assault force opened up on his position with automatic weapons. Bolan could hear the rounds strike his vehicle while others zinged overhead or slapped the muddy access road that led from the mill to the asphalt a quarter-mile away.

Bolan ripped the HK53 and .44 Magnum Desert Eagle and holster from the trunk. He also managed to acquire the last trio of M-67 grenades attached to his LBE before he rolled away from the vehicle and into the encroaching darkness of the woods that lined the road. Bolan slid into the LBE harness and clipped the military webbing belt around his waist. He then brought the HK53 into battery and slapped the ammo pockets to inventory his rounds. He came up with four 30-round magazines plus the one in the weapon, which he estimated as still half full. It would be more than enough.

The Executioner moved twenty yards deeper into the woods and crouched. The sounds of weapons fire had died away on the chill night. Bolan thanked his good fortune that he happened to be wearing fairly dark clothes. He heard a shout and a moment later the crash of boots invading the woods on every side. Bolan estimated they had sent at last half of their force to find him. He knew the other half would set up a perimeter in case he tried to double back and escape.

Bolan took a position against the cold and unyielding bark of a thick tree and pulled an M-67 free. He yanked the pin, let the spoon fly and immediately tossed the bomb as hard as he could to his rear. The tree served as cover from the brilliant flash of the high-explosive filler. The explosion rocked the trees around him, sending flashes of hot gas whooshing past him on either side. The explosion died as the screams of a couple of men crescendoed.

Bolan broke cover and moved on a lateral line to flank the enemy's position. In the twilight he spotted the shadows of one man crashing through the woods on an obvious mission to seek out and destroy Bolan. The Executioner raised the HK53 to gut level and triggered two short bursts, both of which contacted the target. The man let out a shout of pain and surprise as the first rounds grazed him, and then he dropped suddenly from sight, having taken the second burst full in the chest. A second gunner nearby spotted the muzzle-flash from Bolan's weapon and triggered his own volley, but in his excitement the man's aim went high and wide.

Bolan crouched in the foliage and maneuvered to a new firing position. His boots crunched over the dried pine cones and dead twigs and branches from the trees overhead. Bolan took solace in the fact it wasn't late enough in the year for all the trees to have totally shed their summer greenery, which helped to provide some concealment from his enemy. He stuck his head above the low brush of a wild hedge, but his opponent had changed positions. Bolan considered his options but quickly ruled out the use of a grenade or indiscriminate fire. He didn't necessarily stand a chance of hitting his enemy with either, which left only the likelihood of revealing his position.

Bolan remained crouched and waited. In a scenario like this, survivability usually went to the one who could remain still and quiet the longest. The soldier's ploy paid off, for within a few minutes one of his enemy shifted position and made enough noise for Bolan to pinpoint his location. The Executioner laid his weapon between the notches of two branches sprouting from a young sapling and aimed his muzzle in the direction of the noise. He squeezed the trigger for delivery of a sustained burst. His rounds found flesh and a scream rewarded his efforts.

The Executioner changed positions, a move that saved his life as at least three other enemy gunners opened up on where he'd stood just a millisecond before. Bolan noted the position of the muzzle-flashes as he charged into a flanking position, his movements undetectable in the retorts of autofire from three different weapons. Once he was satisfied with his position, he armed another M-67 and tossed it into the approximate center of the triangle of muzzle-flashes. The grenade exploded as the weapons fire died. The flash lit up the woods, and in that brief instant Bolan could see all three of the shooters were caught in the effective range of the M-67.

Bolan turned and headed deeper into the woods before turning in a direction that would take him farther from the mill but parallel to the road. Bolan remembered that after about fifty yards there was a sharp bend in the roadway that would allow him to approach the SUV crew from the rear and increase his chances of taking them by total surprise. When he'd traveled a sufficient distance, Bolan turned once more and again headed for the road. He moved quickly but quietly, stopping every few yards to listen for sounds of pursuit.

Finally, Bolan emerged onto the road to find complete darkness had settled upon him. He moved along the shoulder, keeping to the wood line and ready to seek its shelter and protection at any moment. He completed traversing the bend and came on the SUV crew whose backs were to him, save for the driver's. Bolan crouched and took an inventory. One sat smoking while the other stood just outside the open door of his vehicle, apparently keeping vigil on the woods where Bolan had first disappeared. Two more were standing at the open passenger's door of MacDermott's truck. One appeared to be supervising the other, who seemed to be searching under the seat.

Two more were too busy searching Bolan's sedan to notice much. The Executioner formed a quick plan of attack, settled on a course of action. He shed the LBE, military web belt and HK53, armed and palmed the last M-67 in his left hand and then drew the Beretta 93-R with his right and launched into a sprint from his crouched position. Bolan waited until he was within twenty yards before he raised the Beretta and fired. He triggered a round, and the subsonic 9 mm Parabellum slug took the watchful driver in the head with a pinpoint accuracy that reflected Bolan's reputation as an Army marksman. The round blew off the top of the man's skull and sent him crashing into the weeds.

Bolan turned his weapon toward the driver still seated in the SUV at the same time he tossed the grenade gently over the roof of the vehicle. A complete look of surprise overcame the driver, and the cigarette fell from his mouth a heartbeat before Bolan sent a bullet through the open window of the passenger's door. The bullet entered just below the driver's right cheek and blew bone fragments and brain matter through the driver's-side window.

The grenade landed on target and rolled to the feet of the pair standing next to MacDermott's truck. Bolan threw himself against the body of the SUV for cover just a moment before the grenade exploded. The impact shook his teeth and rattled his eardrums as the heavy whoosh of superhot gases and metal fragments shredded flesh from bone and blew appendages from the trunks of the pair.

Bolan rolled to his feet and came around MacDermott's truck on the passenger's side. He could see the outlines of the spider-webbed windshield—it told him all he needed to know about

MacDermott's condition. Bolan continued to his sedan and caught the two men who had been searching his car just as they extracted themselves from the front and back seats, respectively. Bolan took the rear-seat guy first, since he was closest, with a double-tap to the chest. The impact slammed the guy against Bolan's sedan before he crumpled to the dirt road in a bloody heap. Bolan swung the muzzle onto his second target, who was clawing for hardware beneath his bulky jacket. The man's awkward response cost him his life as Bolan took him with a single shot to the head before the guy managed to clear his pistol.

Bolan spun and came to a complete standstill, his Beretta now aimed toward the wood line. He waited a full minute—willed his breathing and heart rate to slow—waited for any further resistance to present itself. Nothing. No sound of footfalls, no movement from the brush, no shadowy outlines. His ears rang but Bolan's combat sense remained at full alert, prepared to counter anything the enemy might try to throw at him.

Still nothing.

Bolan lowered his pistol and marched to MacDermott's truck. He looked through the tinted window, the cab illuminated by the open door on the other side. He didn't have to open the door to make out the spatters of blood against the back and driver's-side windows. MacDermott's head hung to one side, and Bolan could make out the faintest hint of steam as it wisped from the passenger's door.

Damn.

This was what he'd hoped to prevent more than anything else. Fagan MacDermott, whatever else he may have been, hadn't deserved to die like this. And if Bolan didn't do something about this now, take the fight to Gowan, it would only get worse.

Bolan turned and searched the bodies but didn't find any identification. That seemed a little too strange to him. He would have expected Gowan's men to be carrying something: wallets, money, some kind of business cards. But none of these characters had a thing on them. Another thing he noticed was their weapons.

These crews were carrying an assortment of vintage weapons, some AK-47s, one modified SKS. One even had an old M1911 A-1, Vietnam era. These weren't the weapons of a well-equipped killing team from Mickey Gowan. No, this meant something else entirely. No way had Gowan sent this crew to do in Mac-Dermott. Plus, this was way too soon. Gowan would have only gotten the news right about now, just like MacDermott said.

That left just one explanation: Earth Liberation Front. The ELF terrorists had made their second move. Apparently, they had grown tired of waiting and they were planning to take back what was theirs. Bolan just hadn't expected them to act this soon. It no longer looked as if he could afford to wait and execute his plan. He stood on the edge of an all-out war right here in Timber Vale, and that left him with one choice.

It was time for the Executioner to launch his counteroffensive.

12

Bolan decided that taking his rental sedan would pose a risk. Too many people knew the vehicle on sight, and he didn't doubt for a second that if Gowan's people hadn't already tried to make their move they would real soon.

He retrieved his weapons and stored them beneath a blanket in the backseat of one of the SUVs, then drove back to the mill. Using the key he lifted from MacDermott's pocket, Bolan accessed the storage room. He removed the backseat from the SUV and quickly loaded all of the ordnance and as many of the weapons as he could. The cache included civilian market AR-15 carbines, thousands of rounds of .223 ammunition and even an M-60 machine gun. The rest of the stock was pistols of various makes, including SIG-Sauers, Berettas and Smith & Wessons. Bolan piled the rest of the weaponry in the chipping pit, wired it with some of the demolitions and blew it to scrap metal with a remote detonator as he drove away. Fortunately, the remoteness of the mill had apparently prevented anyone from hearing the explosions and gunfire—not that either would have seemed totally out of place given the mill regularly used ordnance.

Bolan drove the SUV into town and parked down the street from a local bed-and-breakfast being used as a temporary base of operations for Flannery and his crew. In this case, it had turned out to be the most convenient, since it happened to be run by Flannery's mother, not to mention the poetic justice served in the fact one of Gowan's cronies had written the original financing loan. Flannery's family, however, eventually bought out Mickey

Gowan from a settlement they received related to the death of Flannery's father in a logging accident, so now they owned it free and clear.

The Executioner had little to fear from the local police at this point, since it was doubtful anyone would miss the ELF crew for a while and less likely that the vehicle would be reported as stolen. Not to mention the rumors that half the force, including the chief, skimmed funds from Gowan's graft anyway. Hence, Bolan figured he had a few hours before things went really hard, and that would buy him all the time he needed.

Bolan watched the bed-and-breakfast for nearly a half hour before he decided to risk a visit. He crossed the street, ascended the steps to the front stoop and rang the bell. An older woman with dark, curly hair streaked with gray answered the door. Bolan could see the family resemblance to Flannery immediately.

He nodded in greeting and asked for Flannery. The woman harrumphed an acknowledgment, raised a finger to indicate he should wait and then closed the door in his face. Bolan studied his surroundings while he waited on the stoop, watchful for any observers, but nothing stood out. The street seemed quiet—almost too quiet. A sensation tickled Bolan's nape, a pinprick feeling that something seemed out of place, but he still didn't see anything.

Flannery opened the door a moment later. He looked behind him and then stepped onto the porch and closed the door behind him. He didn't look happy to see Bolan.

"What the hell you doing here? You're supposed to be with Mac."

"Mac's dead."

Flannery's voice was edged like cold steel. "What?"

"Somebody ambushed us as we were leaving the mill."

"And they killed Mac," Flannery replied, the accusation obvious in his body movements. "But *you* managed to get away."

"Barely," Bolan said. "There were a lot of them."

"Gowan's men?"

"Yeah, I'd guess so."

Flannery snorted in way of reply. "You'd *guess* so?"

"Listen, don't start with me," Bolan said. "We all knew Gowan was playing for keeps, so this shouldn't come as any surprise to you."

"It don't make sense," Flannery said. "How could he have found out so soon?"

"Obviously someone in your little group betrayed us," Bolan said.

Bolan knew the statement wouldn't sit well with Flannery, but he didn't care right at the moment. He needed the guy off balance and mistrustful of everything and everyone. That would make him less likely to act rashly. He wasn't as controlled and calculating as MacDermott. Flannery would figure it was time to take action and go off half-cocked, which was why Bolan had removed all of the armament from the mill and destroyed what he couldn't take with him.

Flannery cursed and spit over the railing. "That's it, then. Mickey's given us his answer by drawing first blood."

"I think you ought to wait it out a little longer," Bolan said.

"I don't give a shite what you think, Cooper!" Flannery stood more erect in an attempt to look bigger and tougher than he really was, although he'd learned from earlier experience not to touch Bolan. "I don't take orders from you. In fact, *I'm* in charge now that Mac's gone."

"Some of the others might think differently."

"Then they can kiss my ass, too. Now I'm only going to tell you this once. Get the fuck out of here and don't come back. See? If you do, I'll waste you on the spot."

"That's the way you want it," Bolan said.

"Yeah. That's the way I want it."

Flannery turned, went inside and slammed the door on Bolan. The Executioner stood there another moment and stared at the door, considered whether he ought to kick it in, but decided it wasn't worth it. He couldn't do any good for Timber Vale by turning this into a pissing contest on the personal level. He didn't like Flannery and he didn't trust him, but he didn't need the guy to protect the others and he preferred to work alone anyway. So what difference did it make?

As Bolan turned on the stoop and started down the steps, he heard a vehicle approach to his left. His eyes flicked toward a silver-gray Town Car and then caught the flash of a streetlight on metal as the barrel of a gun protruded from the window. Bolan never heard the shot, but there was no mistaking the whine of bullets past his head or the slap of their impact on the bricks. The Executioner leaped over the railing to his left and dropped past the sidewalk into a stairwell that led to a basement access beneath the ground floor of the B and B. He missed one of the steps by mere inches, a saving grace that surely would have broken his ankle if he'd landed any other way.

Bolan brought out the Beretta, raced up the steps and whipped around the railing to see the taillights of the streaking Town Car. He dropped to one knee, sighted down the slide as he thumbed the selector to 3-round-burst mode and squeezed off two sets. The first triburst sparked off the asphalt, but the second series smacked the tires and caused a blowout. That wouldn't have normally stopped the vehicle, but because the Town Car happened to be in midacceleration the sudden loss of traction put the vehicle in a spin. The tail swung in an arc and contacted another car parked at the curb, which brought it to a halt with a screech of rubber on pavement and the crunch of metal and fiberglass.

Bolan got to his feet and quick-stepped in the direction of the vehicle as he changed the selector switch to single shot and scanned the site with the muzzle of his weapon in a search for targets. The driver's door opened and the occupant went EVA as he clawed inside his jacket for hardware. Bolan never slowed pace as he triggered two rounds, the first hitting the driver in the chest center mass and the second punching through his throat. The impact lifted him off his feet and slammed him against the Town Car.

The passenger jumped from the vehicle and fired a volley that sent the Executioner diving for cover behind a nearby parked car.

He could hear the ratcheting echo of the bolt and determined in a heartbeat his opponent held a sound-suppressed SMG. Even the Executioner wouldn't stand a chance against that kind of fire-power with the Beretta as his only weapon. Bolan counted to three and then beelined from the car and toward the SUV, where he could procure firepower to even the odds. He sprinted as sparks flew around him and autofire ricocheted off the pavement.

Bolan made the corner of the building and didn't slow a moment as he dashed for the SUV. He climbed behind the wheel and gunned the engine, then swung the vehicle into a U-turn and tromped the accelerator. Bolan jerked the wheel hard to the left and almost rounded the corner on two wheels. He steered out of the pending fishtail and then leaned out the window with his HK53 and triggered a sustained burst at the Town Car to keep heads down during his approach. Sparks showered the front of the vehicle, chopped the engine to scrap metal and turned the wind-shield into a cracked-ice mosaic. Bolan stood on the brakes and brought the nose of the SUV to a halt inches from the Town Car.

Bolan rolled from the SUV as the passenger stuck his weapon over the hood of the Town Car and blindly triggered a burst that completely missed Bolan's vehicle. The Executioner followed through to his feet and came up on the passenger's side of the Town Car, HK53 held at the ready. The passenger looked at Bolan and expressed utter shock a heartbeat before he tried bringing an MP-5 K to bear. The Executioner triggered the HK53 and dispatched his enemy with a half-dozen rounds.

Bolan spun on his heel and returned to the SUV. He backed out of his position and then put the vehicle into a one-eighty. The door to the B and B swung open as Bolan drove past and a half-dozen of Flannery's goons spewed forth, an assortment of pistols and shotguns held at the ready. Bolan thought they almost looked comical. They were a motley bunch, to be sure, but what they had in enthusiasm they lacked in experience. They didn't stand a chance against either the ELF or Gowan's men.

The Executioner took a corner at the end of the street and

headed for the roadside motel he'd picked to be an alternate base of operations. He didn't want to risk returning to the first one. This way, he could park the SUV in the back and work on his newly acquired armament without interruption. The place had been totally vacant early that morning, and since this was the off-season for tourists he could rely on a modicum of privacy.

Bolan had little doubt this encounter had been with a couple of Gowan's crew. They hadn't exactly sent the best of the lot so far, first letting one lone female FBI agent get the better of them, then allowing Bolan to escape two separate hit attempts. Bolan knew he possibly wouldn't escape a third. Unless he was stupid, Gowan would send his very best next time.

Fine.

Mack Bolan would be ready.

THE ROAR OF THE VAN ENGINE resounded so loudly in Newbury's ears she didn't remember hearing the whip-crack reports from her Glock 19 as she triggered round after round at the vehicle bearing down on her.

Nothing in Newbury's training could have prepared her for such an encounter, and she knew only pure adrenaline motivated her now as the weapon rocked in her grip with each successive pull of the trigger as she lay down a ceaseless barrage of fire.

At the last second, Newbury dived toward the shoulder of the road. She gritted her teeth as the rough ground chewed at the skin beneath her clothes and the gravelly surface left abrasions on her elbows, stomach and knees. Newbury rolled out of the dive and came up on one knee. The van whooshed past and skidded to a halt some twenty yards from her position with its rear doors facing her. The doors broke open a moment later and a pair of black-clad figures jumped from the back, silhouetted against the lit interior.

Newbury took up a two-handed shooting stance and let loose with a failure drill volley—a common live-fire exercise where a double-tap to the chest failed and the shooter had to follow with a third shot to the head. All three rounds connected, and the man staggered backward and fell partially into the van before sliding off the floor and face-first to the ground. Newbury lined up her shot on the second man, but a moment too late as she spotted a small flash in his hands. The expected burn of the bullet entering her body, the trauma of dying thoughts, never came. Instead she felt an electric shock go through her body. Her weapon fell involuntarily from her grasp, and she tasted the saltiness of blood where she'd bit her tongue before the picture before her eyes took on the aspect of a photographic negative and she went to her knees.

Then her world went black.

NEWBURY WOKE WITH A START and realized only a minute or two had elapsed since she lost consciousness.

The bright spots around her eyes dissipated, replaced by the face of Jeff Kellogg staring down at her. "Wake up, sunshine!"

"You traitorous bastard," she muttered through the thickness. "I ought to kill you."

Kellogg snorted. "Doubtful! You're in no position to make good on such a threat, not to mention the fact I knew you were following me."

"Sure, you did," Newbury said, sneering. She tried to kick him in the face, but her leg rose only partway before something jerked on it. She lifted her head, a move that caused so much nausea she felt like puking right there, and saw they had manacled her feet to the floor of the van.

"Oh, you must be referring to the fact you were actually following two men who were following me," Kellogg said, looking nonchalantly at his fingernails. "Yeah, I saw them, too. What's wrong with you, Sandra? You think I joined the FBI yesterday or something?"

"You have no business being in the FBI." Newbury spit at him, but she missed and got a slap across the face for her troubles, hard enough to rattle her teeth.

"You're right! They don't pay well enough!" Kellogg looked

at the trio of armed men in the back of the van with him and all of them burst into laughter.

Newbury remained straight-faced as she replied, "Wherever you're taking me you won't get far. The office knows I'm following you, and they'll send someone after me."

"Don't bullshit me, Sandra. You're dealing with a master of deception. You and I both know nobody's coming after you because they didn't know you were following me. You see, nobody in authority would have given the okay to tail me unless you had substantial proof of wrongdoing, and since you haven't been here long enough to know your ass from a hole in the ground, let's not pretend like someone was just going to hand you such a sensitive investigation carte blanche."

"Matt Cooper knows where to find me."

"Oh, really? This wouldn't be the same Cooper you accused just this morning of kidnapping and holding you against your will, would it? Well, you won't have to worry about that because Matt Cooper's dead."

"I don't believe you."

"Fine, don't," Kellogg said, waving the matter away. "It doesn't matter anyway, since he doesn't know where you are. Nobody knows where you are, and nobody's going to come rescue you. Why don't you just admit I'm smarter than you are and accept your fate?"

"And what's that?"

Kellogg smiled but it lacked warmth; in fact, his smile chilled her to the bone. "Do you really have to ask?"

Newbury put on her toughest mask. "Why don't you give it up, Kellogg? All you have against you right now is kidnapping a federal agent. Do you really want to add murder to that? Is it worth it?"

"You assume they'll catch me."

"They will."

Kellogg looked bemused. "What makes you think so?"

"Maybe there's nothing I can do about you," Newbury countered. "But I don't believe Cooper's dead. I sense he's still out there. And if he is, you can believe he's going to come after you and kill you."

"Don't hold your breath," Kellogg said with a chuckle, although he seemed less confident now. "If the little strike team my friends here sent to Timber Vale doesn't do the job, then I'm sure Gowan's people will."

Newbury nodded in understanding. "Yeah, I get it. You've been playing both sides of the fence. And I know exactly who your 'friends' are, Kellogg. You're in way over your head, which just demonstrates your stupidity even more."

"Shut up, you bitch!" Kellogg said and he slapped her hard once more.

A hand came out to restrain Kellogg's as he wound up for another strike. That hand belonged to one of the three men in the van dressed in their woodland-pattern camouflage. "That's enough."

"You don't tell me what to do," Kellogg snapped.

"Maybe not," he said. "But my orders were to take her alive at all costs, and that's what I intend to do."

Kellogg answered the challenge with a hard stare but kept his peace. Well, for the moment Newbury would be okay. Kellogg apparently answered to a higher authority whom she hadn't met. Maybe she could convince whoever was in charge that holding her hostage wasn't such a good idea. Not that it made a bit of difference, since she planned to do everything possible to escape. While she'd put up a good front, she couldn't be the least bit sure Matt Cooper would find her or if she'd still be alive on the off chance he did.

13

If the men hadn't been part of Gowan's personal crew, and Parrish hadn't been trying to impress the boss with his fealty, Struthers Sullivan would have killed them all.

"You shouldn't have done it, Arty." More quietly he added, "This kind of thing isn't your line of business. I told you to just find him and then leave the rest to me."

"Sorry, Sully," Parrish replied. "I'm *really* sorry. Okay? I wasn't trying to step on your toes or nothing. I was trying to do what you told me. The boys just got carried away."

Sully found it difficult to get mad at the guy. He'd known Artus Parrish too long to question the guy's intentions. Parrish had always proved dependable in most any situation.

"I hope you understand now why Mickey sent me to take care of this. Personally."

"Yeah," Parrish replied sullenly. "I understand."

"Good. Then we forget about what happened. If anybody asks, it was all this Cooper's doing. Got me?"

"Yeah, Sully, I got you."

With the formalities dispensed with, Sully considered his next move. He didn't want to admit they were possibly up against a more formidable opponent than ever before, but the thought of such a challenge intrigued him too much not to pursue the idea. Sully had never gone up against a man like Cooper.

"Everything this guy does is calculated," he told Parrish. "Cooper seems to plan it all out to the last detail. He's not just some hired gun."

"He's like a soldier," Parrish interjected. "Like some kind of robotic war machine."

"That's it!" Sully said with a clap of his hands. He stood and looked into through the window of the office, which had closed for the night, leaving only himself, Parrish and a trio from Parrish's crew who sat outside the office playing solitaire. The streets were practically deserted, and it was barely 9:00 p.m.

Minutes before they had received the call about the failure of Parrish's men to kill Cooper, Gowan had called to tell them Mac-Dermott had announced a full strike would begin at midnight and would effectively close down half the businesses in town, including the mill. Gowan had made it clear that Sully needed to "deal with that shithead MacDermott and anybody else who doesn't work for me anymore."

So far, Parrish's crew hadn't been able to locate Fagan Mac-Dermott or any of the other business owners in league with the union leader. They did know that Cooper had visited Chep Flannery at the bed-and-breakfast.

"So what do you want to do about Flannery?" Parrish asked.

"Nothing," Sully replied. "We need to sit on this until the cops clear out of the area."

"You think they'll have the B and B watched?"

"No," he said. "At least not too closely if we tell them not to. But I don't want to chance anything right now. I'd prefer they think we aren't connected to this. Keep the heat off Mickey's neck."

So all Sully could do now was sit and think about his next move. And before he could do that, he had to figure out how Cooper would be playing this.

"Let's think carefully about this, Arty. There's no doubt in my mind that Cooper's been working his own game *inside* of Mac-Dermott's little crowd, and that has obviously drawn the attention of not only the ELF but many of our friends inside the local law. Jeff Kellogg said as much, and while I no longer trust his loyalty to Mickey I do believe his information regarding the cops and their take on Cooper."

"Which is?"

"They see him as a menace, and I think we can use that to our advantage. You see, I still have certain contacts at a number of levels with people who serve their masters in much the same way I serve Mickey, and I have a feeling they will do their best to stop Cooper from conducting any more of his violent activities, never mind the fact they know who I work for and would be just as anxious to take down the Gowan Family. In this way, we can throw them a bone."

"You think they'll help you?"

Sully nodded. "I believe so. Especially when they understand that we're both after the same thing. This will neatly put an end to Cooper's disinformation campaign. Otherwise, Mickey stands to lose a very large number of his investments and the ELF's money right along with them. He's already sending some additional crew up to help protect the investment, but he was pretty clear this doesn't absolve me of making sure we put Cooper six feet under."

"That wouldn't do us well with them, eh?"

"Now you get the picture."

"So we do it your way, of course," Parrish said. "But once we get the cops to flush this guy like a rabbit from a hole, what then?"

"Then we send in the dogs," Sully replied with a wicked grin.

MACK BOLAN PREPARED for his next move: all-out war with Gowan's soldiers.

Gowan would undoubtedly be sending an army into Timber Vale, and he'd basically taken the town's only defense. It was better that way. Most of these people didn't have the first clue what it would take to fight this kind of war. Gowan's men wouldn't show any remorse about gunning down innocent people, and Bolan knew the local police force wouldn't help.

Bolan inspected the AR-15s he'd confiscated from Fagan MacDermott's weapons cache. They were single-shot repeater rifles, which wouldn't do Bolan a whole lot of good despite the fact they could handle either the ammo boxes full of .223 or the scant few magazines that remained of 5.56 mm NATO rounds for his HK53. Bolan decided to let the latter remain his primary weapon and keep a couple of the AR-15s with full 20-round magazines on hand in the event he needed a backup. The Beretta 93-R and .44 Magnum Desert Eagle were in their customary places, and Bolan toted plenty of spare ammo for each.

As Bolan prepped two of the AR-15s, he considered the most likely approach Gowan's men would take. They would by now have realized that this wasn't going to be any conventional hit. Bolan would be ready and willing to receive them, but they knew that and would be more watchful and cautious.

IT DREW FROM EVENING to late at night, and finally to early-morning hours before Bolan's "wait until you see the whites of their eyes" strategy paid off. He sat in the dark at a small table beneath the casement window that afforded him a view of most of the parking lot and the highway beyond it through the gap between the curtain and window. The single streetlight illuminating the lot wasn't bright enough to betray Bolan's position.

First he heard the crunch of the tires on gravel, and then he saw the black Ford Expedition as it rolled slowly past his window with its lights off. The vehicle continued another ten feet before the engine died. A second, identical vehicle rolled in a moment later and took up a position just short of Bolan's window, and he then saw a sedan pull to the side of the road at the edge of the small gravel lot.

No way were these terrorists or hired guns. Yeah, Bolan had seen this drill more times than he could count. Definitely cops.

Bolan considered his options at this point in the game. He'd always sworn not to drop the hammer on a good cop, and he wasn't about to start now. Fortunately, he'd requested the room on the end that just happened to have two exits, the guest door and a service access that led through the maid closet and then outside to the rear where he'd parked the SUV. If he timed it right,

Bolan figured he could slip out the back and be gone before they could respond.

The Executioner watched silently as the cops went EVA and converged on his door. A number of them were wearing vests, and Bolan caught the flash of yellow FBI lettering on the back of one of the men. Maybe these were friendlies sent by Newbury, but somehow Bolan didn't think so. Why not just knock? Kellogg had either convinced her that Matt Cooper spelled big trouble or Kellogg was operating on his own. What Bolan couldn't figure was how they'd caught on to him so quickly. He'd been careful that nobody followed him, although there wasn't really any fool-proof way of shaking observers. Still, Bolan had been at the game long enough to know most of the tricks, and he was certain that nobody had followed him.

Bolan rose and started for the back door when the flash of the streetlight reflecting off another car stopped him in his tracks. Headlights on the silver BMW winked out as the car pulled off the road and parked directly behind the government sedan. This gave the Executioner pause. Unless the government had started issuing luxury sedans to their supervisors or the director of the FBI had brought his personal vehicle, Bolan didn't figure those as law-enforcements types. Bolan figured his case was made when four men in suits exited from the BMW—no way were they cops. Bolan had to congratulate Gowan's people. Use subtlety and some cash under the table to get the cops to find him and then make sure Bolan wound up cold and dead on a slab at the local morgue. Convenient and neat, and nobody would ask any questions. The cops could tell the press they had caught the man responsible for the "crime spree" going on in Timber Vale and it would all fade into a distant memory.

Well, Bolan still didn't plan on killing cops. He needed to take this to another place. Too bad he didn't get the chance.

As the FBI and SWAT officers got into position and Gowan's crew drew its pistols but kept a respectable distance to watch the show, the dynamics of the situation changed entirely. Several familiar-looking SUVs seemed to materialize out of the darkness and skidded to a halt in the parking lot. Heavily armed men and women in camouflage fatigues and toting automatic rifles leaped from the vehicles and opened up on the cloistered federal posse.

Bolan threw himself to the floor as the wild rounds shattered the glass to the motel-room window or ripped through the paper-thin walls and door. Bolan crawled to the service door and managed to make the rear exit. The sound of autofire being traded between the parties continued as Bolan climbed behind the wheel and fired the engine. Bolan backed out of his space and jerked the wheel to swing the nose into position. He dropped the selector into drive and tromped the accelerator. Gravel sprayed up and struck the undercarriage with the tinkling of rock on metal as Bolan rounded the side of the motel and pointed the hood straight for the center of the carnage.

He saw that about half of the federal agents had already fallen under the onslaught of the new arrivals. Bolan gritted his teeth as he headed straight for the lead SUV. There would be no more dead cops on his watch if he had anything to say about it. And he did. Bolan slammed his SUV into one of the enemy vehicles and then swung his HK53 out the open window and laid down a high-velocity firestorm. One of the female ELF terrorists took a full burst to the chest that knocked her off her feet. Her head slammed awkwardly against the SUV and left a splattered mess of blood before her body hit the ground.

Bolan dispatched two more terrorists with short bursts at center mass. The 5.56 mm slugs ripped ventilated the chest of one, perforating heart and lungs, and dumped him prone to the gravel lot. The other caught three rounds to the skull, one that ripped away the better part of his jaw while the other pair cracked his skull wide open and made mush of his brains.

Another terrorist managed to flank Bolan's SUV from the passenger's side and rushed to finish the job but the Executioner reacted with all the expected speed and accuracy of a combat veteran. The Beretta filled his right fist, and he triggered a 3-round burst through the open passenger's door window. The rounds struck the enemy gunman's chest, neck and head with force enough to drive him back and decide the victor of the contest with finality.

Bolan jumped from the SUV and sprinted toward the second enemy vehicle. The terrorists were just outside their SUV trading shots with the crew using the BMW for cover, and they weren't aware of the new threat approaching. The driver had to have sensed Bolan and performed a right sweep with the muzzle of his weapon as Bolan got close. The Executioner kept forward motion and whipped the stock of the HK53 into the terrorist's head, striking his temple. The blow dropped the man where he stood.

Bolan cleared the driver's door and triggered a burst that took out a female terrorist standing outside the open front passenger's door just as she swung the muzzle of her SMG in his direction. A volley of high-velocity rounds caught her in the midsection, and she hit the ground hard. Bolan jumped into the driver's seat and found the engine running. He shifted into reverse and popped the clutch as he smoothly depressed the accelerator. The vehicle lurched backward and the pair of rear open doors clipped the remaining pair of terrorists from that vehicle.

Bolan powered the SUV into a J-turn, double-clutched into second as he skidded to a halt and then roared away from the scene. Only a couple of terrorists were still standing, and as the Executioner blasted away he could see they had dropped their weapons and were surrendering under the approach of a half-dozen police. Bolan saw the briefest flash of recognition from one of the men near the BMW. He filed that description into memory as he quickly fled the scene.

14

While he drove in the direction of downtown Timber Vale, Bolan retrieved one of the two personal cell phones he'd purchased earlier in the week and tried to call Newbury's number. It rang about six times and just as his thumb hovered over the button to end the call he heard a male voice come on the line.

"Who's this?" Bolan asked.

"I think you'd be more worried about why another man's answering Sandra's phone. Wouldn't you?"

Bolan recognized the voice now. "Kellogg."

"Very good," the FBI man replied. "I'm a little surprised to hear you're still alive. I guess we should have given you a bit more credit. You're… Well, I guess the best word would be *resourceful*. Don't you agree?"

"Don't toy with me, Kellogg," Bolan warned.

"Oh, I have no intention of doing that. Instead, I'll come right to the point. Your dear Special Agent Newbury is still breathing, but if you don't back off and forget this whole thing she's going to get real dead in a hurry."

"You kill her and there's no place you can hide."

"Well, that's not true, but I'll go ahead and let you puff up and thump your chest if it makes you feel manlier."

Bolan refused to take the bait. "What did it take, Kellogg?"

"What's that?"

"What did it take to turn you against your country and utterly innocent people? Is money the only important thing left in your miserable existence?"

"Don't try to psychoanalyze me, Cooper." There was no mistaking the warning tone in Kellogg's rebuff. "I've been checked out by the very best shrinks in this country and beaten them at their own game every time."

"I wonder how Mickey Gowan feels about the fact you're in bed with the Earth Liberation Front."

"Gowan's a has-been. His days are numbered just like yours. You can't cheat these people out of millions and not expect repercussions. That's exactly what Gowan's done and now he'll have to reap the consequences."

"Consider Gowan taken care of."

"I was hoping you'd say that," Kellogg declared triumphantly. "You did just what I expected you would and took care of our heavy lifting. Now that the hard part's done, we can focus on our next task. Killing you."

"You've already tried twice and it hasn't worked."

"That's right," he said. "But that's because we haven't dangled the right carrots. You see, I see a pattern in the way you work. In everything you do I noticed you keep away from the general public. You care what happens to the bystanders. It's touching but I'm personally not much for sentiment. That's why I just know when I tell you I have your dear Sandra here that you'll come for her. You won't hesitate for a moment."

"That's where you're wrong," Bolan lied. "She knows the risks and she chose to take them. And I'd be willing to guess right at the moment she's proving to be quite a handful."

Kellogg produced an unfriendly chuckle. "Oh yeah, she's an unfriendly bitch, all right. But nothing I can't handle."

"Why don't you give up the charade, Kellogg?"

"You first," he replied. "I'll tell you what, though. We've decided to give you exactly twenty-four hours to find your little friend. If you can do it then maybe, just maybe, you stand a remote chance of rescuing her alive. Whether she lives or dies makes little difference, since her fate isn't tied to your own. You're going to die no matter what, Cooper."

"We'll see," Bolan replied.

"You can skip the false bravado," Kellogg said. "However, I can honestly say I hope to see you real soon."

"Whatever happens you can bet on one thing, Kellogg."

"What's that?"

"When all this is through, I'm going to make it my personal mission to kill you."

"Sure, you will, Cooper. Sure, you will."

The line went dead with a click in Bolan's ear. He dropped the phone on the seat and cursed but then stopped to consider his options. The cops would have an APB out for his vehicle right now, which meant the Executioner needed to switch out vehicles once more. Good fortune happened to be smiling on Bolan as he noticed he was approaching the road that led to the mill.

Bolan swung onto the access road and killed his lights immediately. He shifted into first gear, crawling along the winding access road until several police units screamed past him on the asphalt. Once they had passed, Bolan turned on his headlights and continued at best possible speed for the mill. He arrived a few minutes later, parked the SUV and checked the back for equipment or additional weapons. None. Well, he still had the spare ammunition for the HK53 and the SSG 300 sniper rifle in the trunk of his rental. Bolan dropped the HK53 in the trunk along with the Desert Eagle. He left the Beretta in place in the shoulder holster but shed the LBE harness he used to tote his knife, garrote and various other tools of war. He foresaw a need to travel a bit lighter coming all too soon.

Once he'd finished, Bolan closed the trunk, climbed behind the wheel and then set off for Timber Vale. Once in town, Bolan found an out-of-the-way pay phone on the wall of a gas station closed for the night. He dropped in change and then dialed a sixteen-digit number from memory. After a series of clicks came a buzzing and then the sound of a fast busy signal. All were standard safeguards Aaron Kurtzman had built into the system. Nearly a minute passed before the Stony Man cybernetics expert's booming but groggy voice came on the line.

"Sorry to wake you," Bolan said.

"It's okay," Kurtzman replied. "What's up?"

"I've got a cell-phone number for you and I need to see if you can pull a trace on its present location."

"This is a GSM-based phone?"

Bolan knew that the Global System for Mobile Communications provided architecture for programmability. As a result, Stony Man's dedicated satellite could pinpoint any GSM-based mobile phone in the world as long as the phone was on; whether the phone had a signal or not became a moot point.

"I assume so," Bolan replied.

Bolan could hear the clack of Kurtzman's fingers as they danced across the keyboard.

"Yeah, there's a GPS unit inside that one, which means I can run a trace and have the location pinpointed for you within the next fifteen or twenty minutes."

Bolan grunted. "Sounds good. I'd appreciate any information you can give me on it and I'm also going to need everything you can get me on a federal agent named Jeff Kellogg, assigned to northern California."

"Will do."

Bolan gave him the number of the temporary cell phone he'd been using and requested Kurtzman send the last-known location via E-SMS, an encrypted form of wireless messaging, as soon as he had it along with the intelligence on Kellogg. Bolan couldn't be sure, but he hoped he might find something about the FBI agent he could use to his advantage. It wouldn't help him locate Kellogg, but it sure might go a long way in predicting his next move or two.

Bolan returned to his vehicle and scanned the deserted street. His car was far enough in the shadows that anyone driving by probably wouldn't see him. He looked at his watch and realized he probably could use a little shut-eye. Bolan primed his inner clock to wake him in exactly two hours and then locked his doors, reclined his seat and drifted into a state of temporary respite.

BOLAN AWOKE WITH a slight start but only darkness and silence greeted him.

He sat up in his seat and checked his watch: 0410. Bolan yawned and stepped out of his car to stretch some of the soreness from his muscles. He wouldn't have minded a cup of coffee to get the juices flowing, but he didn't know if anything other than the Lamplighter would be open and that was probably closed indefinitely given the absence of a cook or waitress.

Bolan got back in his car and started the engine. He cranked the heater to clear the frost that had built up on the windshield and then checked the cell phone. True to his word, Kurtzman had sent the last-known coordinates from the GPS unit in Newburg's phone along with updates on the half hour. According to the readings, Kellogg's position hadn't changed. Obviously, he felt safe where he was and figured he only needed to sit tight and wait for Bolan to arrive. Bolan suspected he'd probably be walking into a trap, but he could turn that to his advantage.

Bolan then looked over Kellogg's dossier, which Stony Man had sent him. The guy had an impressive record. Jefferson Kellogg happened to be a veteran with an impeccable service record, a highly decorated agent and considered sound in mind and body by a score of instructors, mentors and evaluators.

But maybe that's the whole point, Bolan thought.

Kellogg, for all practical intents and purposes, had always done well in everything. That meant with each new achievement people would naturally expect him to exceed his last victory—a vicious cycle that probably kept growing and nagging at him until he could no longer sustain the pressure and collapsed under it.

Yeah, something had just snapped in the guy. Bolan could feel it simply in the way Kellogg had talked and acted over the past few weeks. The guy was short-tempered, irritable and quick to dismiss the suggestions of others. Obviously he'd spent all his time trying to impress other people, sweated through the more difficult times so he didn't let them down, and that led him to believe his way was the only way to succeed. Then when someone like Gowan or whoever in the ELF recruited him, probably men of success who had come by everything easily in life, Kellogg realized he could have all the nice things in life without having to work so hard for them.

Bolan knew this added insight into Kellogg's character wouldn't necessarily translate to absolute victory on the battle-field, but it might go a very long way to predicting Kellogg's actions. In any case, the Executioner concluded Jeff Kellogg was an extremely dangerous individual. Not only had he gone for an indeterminate amount of time working for the ELF while serving on the FBI, but he'd also somehow managed to convince a cunning and experienced crime lord that he bore the sense of false indebtedness. Bolan faced a shrewd, canny enemy.

Bolan reviewed the coordinates again and determined Kellogg was nestled deep in the heart of the Siskiyou Pass approximately six miles east of Highway 273. Bolan listened to his radio for the weather report. It cited some slickness on the roads due to heavy fog, and there was no expectation either would lift for many hours since the weather forecast was for more freezing rain and cloudy skies through that day. That same weather would make his cross-country trek even more difficult.

The other thing concerning the Executioner was his unfamil-iarity with the terrain. It wasn't like Bolan to involve others in his missions but in this case he figured the safest and best bet would be to get some help. He returned the map to the glove com-partment and erased all data history from the cell phone with the exception of the GPS reports, then put the vehicle in gear.

The closest town to where he was headed would be Medford, which he figured he would reach in about an hour depending on fog. Once there, he'd find a sporting goods store and acquire the proper equipment for his jaunt into the mountains. His current attire would never do. He'd need warmer clothes and a good pair of hiking boots, not to mention waterproof bags and climbing equipment like ropes, rappelling gear and a first-aid kit. The most important asset would be locating a guide, someone who knew every bit of that terrain intimately. Bolan figured he'd make those inquiries while in Medford. Surely there would be someone suitable who could help him.

Finding Newbury and taking down the ELF had become his priority at this point. There wasn't any reason to worry about Gowan's crew for a while. Word of the strike, had already been spread so none of the workers would show up to the mill that morning, and Gowan's crew would have a difficult time getting through the Siskiyou Pass under current weather conditions.

Bolan couldn't help but consider the possibility he'd sent Newbury to her death. However, if Kellogg said Newbury was still alive when she wasn't, he wouldn't have had any reason to challenge Bolan to find him.

No, Sandra Newbury was alive and well, although *how* alive and well remained to be seen. In any case, the soldier would try to rescue her. He owed her at least that much. But he'd meant what he told Kellogg about the consequences if he killed her.

Every damned word of it.

15

Sandra Newbury couldn't be sure when darkness faded, but the shafts of light that streamed through the window set high in her concrete cell told her night had given way to dawn.

Her teeth had finally stopped chattering, too.

When they arrived at their destination some time during the night, Kellogg turned her over to a pair of ruffians who dragged her through a large, châteaulike structure and down concrete steps into what looked like a cold and dank basement. They had manacled her to a seven-foot-long slab of concrete that sat maybe two feet off a dirt floor. Only a vinyl mat separated her body from the slab. Newbury could hardly sleep despite her exhaustion. Through the night she dozed fitfully, shivering while curled beneath a thin wool blanket. In the first light she could see it was a very old Army blanket.

Probably dates back to World War I, she thought.

Newbury realized the importance of staying fit and not allowing herself to succumb to the cold, so she climbed from beneath what little warmth the blanket provided and began to do incline push-ups against the slab. She worked hard enough to get her heart rate up some and work the stiffness from her joints and muscles, but not so much that she perspired. She didn't want to risk hypothermia.

She felt better after completing her exercises, then sat on the pad with her knees to her chest and the blanket wrapped around her arms. She couldn't see her breath anymore, a good sign as far good signs went. She guessed that it was somewhere between 0600 to 0800.

Well, at least there didn't remain any doubts in her mind about Jeff Kellogg. Yeah, the guy was as dirty as they came. She couldn't help but be a little angry with herself for allowing Kellogg to capture her. She wondered if he had the guts to make good on his threat to Matt Cooper—she didn't know if Kellogg had the actual guts to murder somebody in cold blood—although she knew that if he was working with the ELF, one of their henchmen wouldn't hesitate to kill her in an instant. Time would tell.

Newbury considered her options. Naturally, she'd do anything she could to escape, or at least make the attempt, if it came to it. FBI agents were taught many of the same techniques the military taught soldiers taken as POWs: don't give any information other than name and rank; don't talk about or answer any questions pertaining to your personal life; don't discuss any current operations; talk as much as possible to those in highest authority or, in other words, don't deal with any lackeys.

That would be easy. Newbury figured Kellogg to be a lackey, so she wouldn't talk to him or answer any questions. She had given careful thought to using her feminine wiles to see if she could sway Kellogg, maybe take him off his guard, but she decided against it. He'd be either too smart or immune to such tactics, since appeals to his ego didn't seem to go far with him. Kellogg had other interests.

Kellogg served a new master now: money.

Newbury took a fair bit of comfort in the fact her situation wasn't entirely hopeless. To keep herself busy, she studied the layout of her cell. Walls of painted concrete rose fifteen feet above her head. The one window providing light was the only one and well out of reach. Aside from the concrete slab there were no other formations or furnishings. The cell had a dank smell to it, and that incessant drip of water seemed to grow louder in her ears, but it didn't reek of sewage. At least she could be thankful for that.

She inspected the manacles on her feet. Twin straps of leather a half-inch thick and about three inches wide encircled both ankles. Thick metal rings were sewn into the leathers through which ran a quarter-inch of forty-grade steel chain. The chain connected to a swivel piece, also steel, the end of which was welded to a ring set in the concrete slab. Newbury looked around her for something she might use to break one of the chain links but found nothing—leave it to her captors to be thorough. Newbury didn't bother continuing with her inspection. She knew it wouldn't do any good. She wasn't going anywhere for the moment. Maybe another opportunity would present itself.

For now she could only wait.

KELLOGG SAT OUTSIDE Percy Jeter's office and cleaned beneath his fingernails with a pocketknife. He was tempted to beat on the door, barge in and tell Jeter exactly what he thought of him, but he knew that wouldn't get him far. He'd brought the information as agreed, but Jeter refused to see him immediately. Apparently his precious sleep was more important than hearing anything Kellogg had to tell him.

It was a quarter to ten before Kellogg finally got in to see Jeter. The old windbag sat in a royal-blue smoking jacket behind a massive desk of hand-carved mahogany. His office was as spacious as the libraries of some smaller towns Kellogg had visited. Books lined wall-high shelves, and all the furnishings looked to be from the Georgian era with its maples and mahoganies and cloths dyed in autumn colors. Kellogg hated this kind of eclectic taste in furniture. The modern glass-and-stainless-steel office suited him much better, but then it didn't matter because he didn't have to work here. And if things went as planned, he would collect the last of his money and be on a plane bound for the Caymans before the sun set.

"Jefferson," Jeter said as he waved toward a chair in front of his desk. "Have a seat."

Once Kellogg was comfortable, Jeter ordered coffee and then picked up a cigar box from his desk and lifted the lid to reveal nearly two full rows of Cuban cigars. Kellogg looked at them a moment with an expression almost as if Jeter had showed him a tin can filled with dead lab mice, then shook his head and sat back in the chair.

Jeter look surprised. "No? A shame, my friend. These are limited-edition Trinidad Fundadores. They produce exclusively for Castro. A friend of mine in the diplomatic corps of the State Department got them for me some time back. A little luxury I afford myself every so often."

"Yeah, seeing as how you're living in such a dump here."

Kellogg saw the suddenly new and dangerous hue to Jeter's skin, but he made no mention of it. Something had put Kellogg in the foulest of moods, and he really didn't feel like being sociable. There would be time for that later. Right now he needed to conduct his business and get the hell out of here as fast as possible.

"I won't mince words, Percy," Kellogg began. "I'm here to give you the information I promised, collect my payment and be on my way."

"Yes, about the payment—"

"Don't try to fuck me over, pal," Kellogg said. "It's been a long night, and it's going to be a longer day. And while I appreciate the hospitality, I'm not interested in sticking around."

Jeter produced a cool smile. "Well, thanks for your candor. And we—that is the Committee—have no intention of fucking you over. We have the agreed price for your information, provided it checks out. All I was about to say is that some things came up, and we were unable to risk transferring the funds to your private accounts as customary, so I'm afraid your final payment will have to be in cash. You don't mind, do you? I didn't figure you would, so I took the liberty of ensuring it's hand delivered to you here today, and I don't mind saying I went to considerable lengths to make it happen. A couple of our members were—how should I say it?—less committed to paying you than others, but I managed to bring them around."

Kellogg nodded as he considered Jeter's announcement. It could be a mere ploy to keep him here, delay him until they could find out everything they needed to know, although he didn't see much sense in that. If they wanted to kill him, they had plenty of opportunities to do it. They could have come in the middle of the night and cut his throat, or simply shot him and buried his body in the woods. Nobody would have ever been the wiser. Instead, they had helped him escape from Gowan's men and assisted with taking Newbury hostage.

Kellogg decided to play it cool and see where things led. "It's fine. I appreciate your vouching for me."

"There is the matter of this woman, though." Jeter relaxed and leaned his elbows on the oversize desk. "You've created a bit of a liability for us. We can't release her without risking significant exposure to our operations here. We've spent too much money and invested too many years keeping this site a secret to now let it unravel because we're squeamish about killing an FBI agent."

"I understand this makes things more complicated," Kellogg said. "But she couldn't be allowed to continue following us, and there was no way to evade her. Bottom line, she cannot leave here alive."

"Oh, I can assure you she won't," Jeter said. "But that, of course, brings us to this other matter of the information you have for us. I do trust after the trouble I've gone to that this is worth it."

"Believe me, it's worth it."

"I'm listening."

"It's time for you guys to act. No more toying with Gowan. His entire organization is about to go down the pisser, and he's vulnerable now. His zombies in Timber Vale have woken up to what's happening around him. There's this guy, Fagan MacDermott, who works for Gowan's mill operations. MacDermott was serving as boss and also union leader."

Jeter nodded. "A conflict of interest if there ever was one."

"Of course it is, but that's the whole point. That conflict has paid off big time for Gowan. Until now. You see, MacDermott got a little too power hungry and decided to make a grab for control of the Timber Vale. It might have worked if he'd done it differently, but MacDermott had a bit of a drinking problem and whenever he got drunk he started running off at the mouth. He trusted the wrong people and it got back to Gowan. You see, Mickey and his boys had always expected this to happen at some point. He just wasn't sure when. But he was always prepared to deal with it when the shit went down."

"I still don't see how any of that is going to benefit us."

Kellogg laughed. "Because something old man Gowan never counted on was how time can build divided loyalties. Some of his people are for him, but a much larger part seeks their independence. The business owners in Timber Vale aren't interested in paying any more graft to Gowan or his cronies. The problem is, however, that money doesn't belong to Gowan and never has. And by the way, that's *your* money he's been playing with."

"What are you saying?" Jeter asked with a sincere look of interest on his face now.

"You don't need to blow up fighter jets and drive business away from Timber Vale. You're working way too hard. All you need to do is lend a helping hand to the good citizens of the town and drive Gowan out of this area for good. You do that, and you're going to be heroes. Then you can easily slide your own folks in to replace Gowan's people. Not only do you get your money back, but you now latch on to an almost endless supply of cash for your other operations."

Jeter nodded in complete understanding now. "And while we're at it, we can take down their mills and eliminate those elements destroying the forests and the air."

"Now you're catching on," Kellogg replied drolly.

"That's an important bonus for us, Jefferson."

"Whatever. So you have the information now. I've got more technical details about when it's all supposed to go down, and we've dealt with the issue of the broad. That having been said, I'd like to know when I can expect my money to be here. I have a plane to catch."

"I should think no later than noon," Jeter said. "It will come with the various members of the Committee."

"I'm not sure that'll work. I have to get to L.A."

"We have a helicopter. I can arrange to have it take you wherever you like. Don't worry, Jefferson. I said I would take care of you, and I intend to keep my word. We may be viewed as terrorists by the outside world, but we're not as barbaric as you might think. We do what's necessary to protect our interests and those of our environment. The difference is that we're not talking about protecting the Earth and then just sitting on our hands like clucking mother hens and doing nothing as the EPA and Greenpeace Foundation do."

"I'm touched," Kellogg said, wondering how much longer he'd be forced to participate in Jeter's self-congratulatory tree-hugger ceremony.

"In the meantime," Jeter continued, "I welcome you to remain here as my guest and avail yourself to some of the finer things. I can arrange breakfast, liquor, just about anything you like. We even keep a complement of female company on the premises just in case." Jeter fired him a knowing wink and added, "I like to be prepared, you know."

"I'm sure. But if it's all the same to you, I think I'll just go watch some satellite and wait for my money to arrive."

Jeter stood to signal the meeting had concluded and reached out his hand. Kellogg took it and shook quickly, then made for the door as fast as possible. Something almost slimy seemed to cling to Jeter's personality. The guy had never been this cordial before, and Kellogg didn't much like it. In fact, he wouldn't have put it past Jeter to try poisoning his food or getting him comfortably nestled in bed with a woman and then having a couple of "soldiers" cut Kellogg's throat while he slept. The sooner he could get out of there the better, although he did keep Jeter's offer of the helicopter in the back of his mind.

After all, there was no reason to be rude.

PERCY JETER PICKED UP the telephone on his desk as soon as Kellogg left the room and dialed the special number. He thought about the FBI agent and felt a pang of regret when he considered how much money they had wasted on the guy. Kellogg was an opportunistic ass and a fool, and Jeter had no tolerance or respect for somebody like that. Their cause deserved better, but they hadn't been able to find any at the time.

"Yes?" a gravelly voice answered on the third ring.

"I assume you know Kellogg showed up last night?" Jeter asked the respondent.

"Of course," the man replied. "I know everything that goes on. *Everything*."

Jeter didn't doubt it. He'd suspected a spy or two among the fighting men and women of the organization. They probably reported everything that transpired. Jeter couldn't stand that kind of activity—he considered it disloyal—but he knew there wasn't much he could do about it. If he made too much noise, the Committee would just find a way to replace him. Jeter liked to believe his influence went far, which it did, but it didn't go *that* far. His number-one mission had always been to make the Committee happy, and that's the only reason he'd advanced as far as he had in the ELF. Like all of them, he served at the Committee's pleasure.

"Then you must also know about the woman."

"Yes."

Jeter sighed. "You want me to take care of it?"

A long silence followed and finally the voice replied, "Yes. She can't leave there alive, and neither can Kellogg. Is that understood?"

"Consider it done."

"Good. Now, what of our other plans? Is everything set?"

"We've had a setback with the weather, but we're monitoring the situation. I expect we should be able to roll out within the next twelve hours. The operation will then proceed exactly as we planned it. It will mean a minor adjustment to our timetable, but we will still accomplish everything we hoped."

"I'm happy to hear that," the man said. "You have done a superb job. If all goes as planned, you may even have secured your place for our next opening on the Committee."

"I'm honored."

"Don't be, you've earned it. We plan to convene our first meeting tonight at your location. Make sure everything is in order."

"We'll be expecting you," Jeter said, but the caller had already hung up.

Jeter replaced the phone in the cradle and sat back in his chair. He looked around the vast expanse of his office for a long time. Finally, he took one of the Cuban cigars from the box and lit it. He ordered a Bloody Mary and then moved from his desk to a nearby leather lounge chair. No point in diving straight into his work. He had only a few phone calls to make that day; he'd cleared the rest of his agenda in anticipation of the Committee members arriving and the beginning of their operation in Timber Vale.

Percy Jeter felt as if he were sitting on top of the world. Finally! This was what he'd worked so hard to achieve: a seat on the Committee. No longer would he have to lick the boots of others, scrounge for the crumbs off their tables like a pathetic dog. Soon *he* would call the shots and make the deals. He would sit in the boardrooms of some of the finest companies in the world and tell the CEOs and directors how things were going to be. The ELF had once been a very small, very influential organization, but all that was going to change. Their demonstration in Timber Vale was only the tip of the iceberg. With that major success they would branch out as they gained more and more supporters, taking hearts and souls of supporters one at a time until they controlled everything and everyone. Then the U.S. government would be forced to listen to them.

Yes, Percy Jeter would be one of the elite few to rule with absolute power over the very water they drank and the air they breathed!

16

According to the Oregon State Rangers Service, the cabin sat at the end of a private road two miles off Highway 273.

"Guy's name is Don Clint," one of the rangers told Bolan. "Best damned guide this side of the Rockies, if you ask me. You plan on doing any hunting?"

"No," Bolan had replied. "Just interested in some hiking. I'm a nature photographer for a Denver tourist magazine."

The rangers had nodded with a glazed interest, the same kind he might have expected if he announced he were a geologist at an after-Oscars party. They gave him the directions, cautioned him to be careful and soon Bolan reached the end of the road. Clint had served as a federal cop with the USDA Forestry Service for almost forty years according to the men at the ranger station, and he'd taken on an almost legendary reputation as a result. Bolan could see why as he climbed from his vehicle.

The man who walked out of the large cabin house sure as hell didn't look seventy. He stood about five foot ten and might have weighed 150 fully clothed. He had watery blue eyes, a shock of salt-and-pepper hair with a matching mustache and beard. A large nose jutted from a face like a rocky outcropping, and he possessed a surprisingly dark complexion. He wore brown wool pants with suspenders and a long-sleeved undershirt. Bolan's immediately spotted the pistol holster riding high on his right hip and the protruding handle of a .44 Magnum revolver.

"Morning," the man said cheerfully. "You lost?"

"No, sir," Bolan said. "Not if you're Don Clint, anyway."

"You must be Cooper."

Bolan smiled. "I take it the rangers called ahead."

"They did." Bolan stopped just short of Clint.

The two men studied each other for a long moment, then Clint held out his hand. "Nice to meet you. Come on inside."

Bolan followed Clint into the cabin, which had the almost expected rustic interior. Clint offered him coffee, which Bolan accepted, and the two sat and made small talk for about ten minutes at a table, the top of which Bolan noticed had been made from the stump of a massive tree. Clint told him the history of the table, how he'd acquired it from a friend when both men worked up in the Yukon.

"You were in Alaska, too," Bolan said, not hiding the surprise in his voice.

Clint nodded and took a swig of coffee. "Yep. Also served in Washington, Oregon, Montana, Idaho and northern Wyoming."

"You've been around, then."

"Yeah," he said with a nod and wistful expression. "Long time."

"You look pretty fit," Bolan noted.

He shrugged, trying to make it look as if he was accepting the compliment gratefully although the Executioner could see it pleased him. "I keep active."

Clint rose and went to his fireplace where he retrieved a large pipe. He filled it with a bit of tobacco from a pouch he kept in the pocket of his wool pants, and then returned to the table before lighting it.

"So," Clint said. "Don't mean to sound rude, guy, but what exactly did you want from me?"

"I need a guide."

"I doubt that," Clint replied with a chuckle. "You look like you've done plenty of this kind of thing on your own. In fact, I'd almost peg you for an ex-cop. You former law enforcement?"

Bolan smiled. "Something like that. Look, I won't insult your intelligence by feeding you some cock-and-bull story. The fact is I'm looking for bad people who've done bad things, including kidnap a young woman. I don't have time to explain a lot of this, but trust me when I say it's of national importance I find this crew."

Clint nodded and let out a deep sigh around the mouthpiece of his pipe. "I figured it was probably something like that. You got an idea where these hooligans might be?"

Bolan brought out his topographical map and showed Clint the last-known location based on Kurtzman's coordinates. Clint looked at it a moment, grunted and then rose and crossed to a very large wooden chest positioned in a corner of the main living area just to the right of a stone fireplace. He opened the lid on creaking hinges and sifted through the contents, setting various items and trinkets along the rim of the trunk carefully until he found what he sought. He replaced all the items to their original places before closing the trunk and bringing a rolled map of old, crinkled paper back to the table.

Clint unrolled the map and Bolan's eyes widened. "The detail on this is amazing. I haven't seen such work even from modern technology. Who was the cartographer?"

Clint laughed and produced a gust of smoke from the bowl of the pipe. "Me."

Bolan realized the reason for Don Clint's legendary status as a forestry officer. "Your reputation is well deserved."

The guy shrugged, but Bolan could tell he appreciated the compliment. He pointed to a section on that map that looked relatively similar to the topographical area Bolan had showed him on the maps developed from satellite reconnaissance of the area.

"Now," Clint began, "if I don't miss my guess those coordinates are about here. You see this ridge right along here? That gives you a pretty decent overlook of the saddle there. The place you're talking about isn't too bad a hike, maybe three miles from here, but the footing is treacherous all the way. I wouldn't try to do it without a fairly decent pack animal like a mountain mule or a donkey. At least something to hold on to and can carry your equipment."

Bolan frowned. "Afraid I'm kind of short on pack animals this trip."

Clint stood erect from where he'd been leaned over the map, pulled the pipe from his mouth, folded his arms and declared, "That shouldn't be too difficult to overcome."

"You've decided to help me, then."

Clint cocked his head. "We'll get to that part in a minute, fella. In the meantime, I can tell you that maybe only a half-dozen people know there's a pretty large private residence nestled in that ridge. Very difficult to see from the air because of the trees, plus the downdrafts there can be somewhat treacherous for your average helicopter. And a fixed-wing plane's out of the question given the narrow ridge walls. Also, there's a lot of evidence of groundwork there, which would suggest to me they produce their own water and power. I can see a well, a sewage field and evidence of maybe a couple underground electric generators."

Yeah, Bolan thought. Sounded like the perfect spot to secret a small army or stash military-grade weapons and explosives. With the ability to fly in food stores and other supplies and not having to rely on road access to deliver utilities, the ELF could turn the place into a veritable fortress if they wanted to *and* provide a secluded training ground.

"You said a private residence," Bolan remarked. "What kind of residence?"

"Big house," Clint replied, "with a helicopter pad and some outbuildings. It actually looks like one of those Swiss ski lodges, you know the kind I mean?"

"A château?"

"Yeah, that's a good word for it. Like a château. I never got too close to that area, since I figured anybody who wanted to build a place in the middle of nowhere like that probably appreciated their privacy, like me. I would have never thought by looking at the place that something illegal might actually be going on."

Bolan nodded. "I bet."

"Which brings me to this helping you. What exactly is going

on in that place? You said they kidnapped a woman. Who's this woman to you?"

"You want to know if this is professional or personal." Seeing no reason not to be straight with the guy, Bolan replied, "The fact is it's a little of both. The woman's name is Sandra Newbury, she's an agent with the FBI. The man who snatched her was her handler until he decided making money was more important than bringing criminals to justice."

"A crooked cop?" Clint said in a loud voice.

"This guy sold out to the Earth Liberation Front," Bolan continued.

"The ecoterrorists. I know their work a little too well."

"I figured you would. Anyway, I think they've been using the place you described as their base of operations. I'm betting that Sandra's there, and I would also bet the ELF's getting ready to deploy their private little army for some nasty business in the town of Timber Vale."

"I've been there lots of times," Clint said. "Nice people there, real nice people."

"Well, they've been pushed around by members of the criminal underworld."

"And you're going to help them push back," Clint said. With a curt nod he spun on his heel and headed for a closet. He pulled it open and triggered a light with the pull of a string dangling from the ceiling. Clint tossed some boots and other miscellaneous items outside the closet, then a rug, before Bolan witnessed him literally seem to pull the floor out of the closet.

Then he stepped into it and began to descend into the floor. Bolan realized Clint had a secret entrance to his crawlspace. The Executioner left his chair, walked to the closet and peered into the opening. About eight steps descended sharply to a wooden deck built over the dirt floor. A moment elapsed before Clint stepped into view and passed two small crates and a long gun case up to Bolan through the opening. Bolan took the offerings and cleared the way for Clint to ascend to the ground floor.

Clint replaced everything exactly as it had been, took some of Bolan's burden and then gestured for him to follow. Clint snatched the map off the table on his way out the door. They left the cabin and proceeded around back, traversing a footpath that led into a wood line. The light beneath the towering mountain pines was feeble at best, and the encroaching darkness seemed even more formidable given the overcast sky. Clint led Bolan along a precarious path that eventually terminated at a small pond.

Bolan almost didn't spot the small corral with a shelter, as the wooden structure had been built in an irregular pattern and stained the color of the trees surrounding it. Beneath the shelter stood a rather large equine with dark, thick fur and long ears. The mule studied Bolan with all the resolute curiosity of the breed, a stare that said to the recipient the animal hadn't entirely made up its mind and would have to give the subject some additional thought.

Bolan shook his head and grinned. "Handsome boy."

"Yup, thanks," Clint replied. He patted the mule on the neck and added, "He can be cantankerous, but most of the time he's gentle."

"Big, too," Bolan noted.

"He's seventeen hands high, which is about as large as his particular stock will go. I named him Mountain."

"I can see why."

Clint opened the gun case and removed a high-powered hunting rifle. He sheathed the rifle in its protective sleeve attached to the nearby leather tack, then stepped inside the corral and expertly saddled Mountain. That chore completed, he opened the crates and withdrew some additional equipment, including a pair of canteens, a web belt stocked with .308 shells for the rifle and a thick hat made of beaver fur. The other crate contained some foodstuffs and rope.

"Why don't you go back to your car and bring down whatever you want to take with you," Clint said.

Bolan nodded and headed back to his car. The numbers were ticking down.

17

"Time to go," Don Clint said.

Bolan nodded his agreement and stepped onto the trail that led up a steep hill. Given the rate of climb along the mountain range and the best possible speed of two men with the mule named Mountain, the Executioner figured two hours was the soonest he could expect to reach his target. He hoped that was soon enough. It wasn't as much the distance they were traveling as the difficult terrain.

The sky remained gray, although as the day wore on the temperature got warmer. During their trek across the peak of the ridge, Bolan heard the rumbling of white water far below, spied the tumble of the creek water over rocks that signaled the first thaws and the imminent arrival of spring. Although the temperature continued to rise, Bolan could feel the cold pinch his nostrils with each breath. He still hadn't grown completely accustomed to the thinner air, so he stopped often to rest and breathe deeply. Despite his excellent physical condition, Bolan knew oxygen deprivation could still occur during strenuous exertion in higher altitudes and he had no desire to succumb to such a malady—not with the stakes this high.

During one pause to rest, Bolan mentioned the distance they covered and Clint pulled the map from where he'd secured it to Mountain's saddle. "I'd say we've gone maybe a mile or so. We're here at this point, on the very peak of the cliff."

"It should be all downhill from here, then," Bolan said. He did nothing to hide the sense of relief in his voice.

"That's when it gets hardest," Clint reminded him. "It's not uphill that's the problem, it's keeping your footing on the way down. And the downhill section of the trail is nothing like what we've encountered until now. The path will narrow by about fifty percent, and we'll start to hit some switchbacks. This is where we'll have to be extra careful, Cooper."

Bolan nodded, fully aware of the grave dangers posed by this little hike. "Let's go," he prompted Clint. "I'm rested."

The two men pressed onward. The first twenty minutes of their descent passed without incident, but their makeshift trail had narrowed just as Clint promised. They were more than halfway down when Bolan took a bad step, got too close to the edge of the cliff and lost his footing. The loose rock and sand gave under his weight, and Bolan had the sense he would fall prior to actually sliding along the sides. At the last moment, he reached out and grabbed a massive outcropping. Bolan wrenched his shoulder a bit in the move, but it saved his life and prevented him from tumbling more than a third of a mile to the saddle floor.

"Hang tight!" Clint ordered.

Bolan had every intention of doing that. He dug his fingers into the protruding rock and held on while watching the activity above his head. He strained shoulder muscles and biceps, attempting to pull his body onto the outcropping, but froze when he heard the crunch of rock and shifting of loose dirt—he also detected a minute shift in its position.

Bolan craned his neck to see the flurry of activity above him. Clint had produced a fifty-foot length of climbing rope. He tied one end to the saddle horn, wrapped the other around a figure-8 ring tied to the animal's tack and then tossed the rope over the edge. It uncoiled as it dropped, and the remainder landed with a dull sound on the outcropping. Bolan kept the fingers of his left hand digging into the rock for support and grabbed the rope with his other. He wrapped the rope around his arm with a few circular motions of his wrist and then grabbed tight and released his hold on the rock. Bolan reached up to grab the rope with both hands and nodded to Clint, who turned and patted Mountain's behind while he made clicking sounds with his tongue. Mountain jerked to a start but then slowly and steadily began to pull Bolan to safety. A minute later, the Executioner stood on solid ground.

"Guess it wasn't a bad idea to bring Mountain along after all," Clint said with a grin.

"I can't argue with that," Bolan replied.

After disentangling his arm from the rope and shaking hands with Clint, Bolan walked to Mountain and patted the animal's neck with a quiet word of thanks. He reached into the bag tied to the saddle and withdrew a fistful of sweet feed. The mule quickly munched at the grain in Bolan's hand; at least a third of it tumbled off the edges of his palm and scattered across the trail.

As the men continued on their treacherous journey, Bolan thought over the roughly sketched layout Clint rendered of the château and surrounding grounds. He'd already begun to formulate a battle plan in his mind, but he wouldn't feel secure in his choice until he got to see the place firsthand. If he faced a large number of combatants, his chances of finding Newbury alive were slim, not to mention there hadn't been time to procure any sort of heavy ordnance. No grenade launchers, no C-4—Bolan had only the HK53, an AR-15 carbine and two pistols. He'd brought the SSG 300, as well, but it wouldn't do him much good in close-quarters combat.

The remainder of their journey passed without incident. The path widened onto a flat plateau high with wheat grass and peppered by trees. Clint left Mountain tied to a tree trunk. He retrieved his Savage Arms 7 mm Magnum rifle from its slipcase and a pair of binoculars, then instructed Bolan to follow. They moved into thicker woods, but Bolan spotted an exit on the other side, visible because of its comparative brightness against the dark woods. Clint signaled they should get low and Bolan complied. A moment later, they crawled from some thickets to the edge of a precipice about a hundred yards above the château.

It stood directly below them, only partially visible through the copse that surrounded it. The walls of the ravine rose along either side like twin guardians. Clint handed the binoculars to Bolan, who studied the general layout and terrain.

"Well, it looks pretty quiet," Bolan finally declared, lowering the binoculars. He passed them over so Clint could take a look. "But that won't make my approach any easier. You see that pair of outbuildings off to the left?"

Clint nodded.

"I'm betting one of them houses the security system."

Clint cast Bolan a sideways glance. "What makes you think so?"

"The antennas and satellite dish on top of the one closest to the main building," Bolan replied. "That's no ordinary satellite TV system down there, believe me. That's state-of-the-art equipment. I've used that stuff before, and I know what it's capable of. I wouldn't doubt it if they weren't already aware of our presence."

"So how do we get inside without being detected?"

Bolan produced a lopsided grin. "Well, *we* aren't going in there—I am."

"So you brought me all this way just to play tour guide. Why? You don't think I can handle myself, fella?"

"No offense, Clint," Bolan replied easily, "and this isn't about your abilities. This has to do with the fact you have no fight with these people, and I'm not willing to risk anybody's neck like that."

"Then what's the point?"

"Come again?"

Clint frowned. "I'm asking you what the point was of being a federal cop all these years, dedicating my life to put criminals behind bars just so I can sit on my sorry ass when something really big goes down. I may be retired, Cooper, but I'm not inept and I'm certainly not disabled. I don't think I got to remind you a young woman's life is at stake here, and you have no idea what you're going to come up against. And no disrespect to *you*, but I was doing this kind of thing before you were born."

Bolan chuckled. "You think so, huh?"

"Young fella, I know so."

Bolan could appreciate Clint's position. The guy was just trying to do what he knew had to be done, and Clint had as much right to participate in this op as Bolan. He'd earned that right when Bolan solicited his help; obviously Clint didn't do anything halfway.

"All or nothing?" Bolan asked, eyeing Clint with an expression of respect.

"All or nothing."

"Fair enough…you're in. But we do this my way."

Clint nodded. "So what's the plan?"

"Well, I'd bet I can get to that perimeter without being detected," Bolan said.

The Executioner had way more experience getting into highly secured facilities than Clint. And while the old cop might be sure-footed, he was still Bolan's senior by a considerable margin, and Bolan could move more quickly and silently than Clint.

Bolan pointed north and continued, "See that ledge over there with the brush? I'm betting that would make a perfect defilade for you to provide me covering fire."

"For what?"

"I thought at first I'd hit them hard and fast, then in the confusion get inside the place and see if I can locate Newbury. Now I'm thinking a soft probe's in order first. That means I still may have to leave in a hurry, and I'd rather have someone covering my back if things go hard. You any good with that rifle?"

"Got my sharpshooter's badge in the Army," Clint replied. "I was always top of the class in my re-quals every year at the Federal Law Enforcement Training Center. And from the distance you're talking it would be like a turkey shoot."

"Let's hope it doesn't come to that," Bolan said.

The two men crawled out of sight and returned to the clearing. Bolan quickly stripped out of his hiking clothes in favor of camouflage coveralls in woodland pattern. He then donned his military web belt with the holstered .44 Magnum Desert Eagle and slid into the shoulder rigging that held the Beretta 93-R. A camouflage hood with a piece that covered his mouth and nose and a Ka-bar fighting knife completed the ensemble.

Bolan slung the HK53. "I'll be back as soon as possible."

"You be careful, Cooper."

"Roger that. Just make sure you're in position by the time I go in or this could go all wrong in a big hurry."

Clint nodded, and Bolan saw the fierce determination in his eyes. He tossed a casual salute to Clint, then turned and headed toward the trail that led to the bottom of the ravine. The stands of trees that surrounded the massive property were thickest on the west side, a fact that would make it much easier for Bolan to approach undetected. Once he got close, though, he'd want to keep his eyes open. All the sophisticated equipment there signaled a pretty advanced electronic setup, and Bolan was certain that the various technologies employed would extend to surveillance and counterintrusion systems.

It still took Bolan nearly forty minutes to reach the perimeter. He crawled the last dozen yards to the perimeter and investigated the expanse. All looked quiet and peaceful, but Bolan had the feeling that was by pure design. Somewhere within that web of deception lay a dormant spider, patiently awaiting her prey to make that one fatal mistake. Bolan knew how such places operated because he'd penetrated those dozens of times before. If the ELF's engineers were really good, they'd have the place wired for sound.

Bolan inspected the perimeter and soon spotted a half-dozen cameras positioned to scan different angles. A bit more time and Bolan noticed they were swiveling on their mounts at regular intervals. So they couldn't cover the entire grounds simultaneously. He studied the movements for a time and built a picture in his mind of a path that would take him through the blind spots.

Bolan peered along the edges of the perimeter, paying particular attention to the corners. He didn't see any electric eyes on pedestals or IR systems at ground level. Such devices were probably not favored here, since they would frequently be tripped by everything from rabbits to deer and elk. The same would hold true for sound systems, since any microphones they placed would not only have to compete with the sounds of nature, but also it would be almost impossible to distinguish between the footfalls of animals and humans.

No, it looked only as if Bolan would have cameras to deal with. The Executioner made one more study of the camera angles and then got to his feet and went to work. He burst into the clearing and ran along the perimeter before turning inward to the center of the grounds and running a zigzag pattern. He reached the rear of a small outbuilding in just under a minute. Bolan put his back flat to the wall, counted to seven and then rounded the corner of the building and continued toward the main house.

As he got closer to his objective, Bolan's senses went on full alert, ready at any moment to hear the shouting of voices or see a small army of ELF terrorists charge from the shadows with autorifles held at the ready. Still, nobody appeared to challenge him, and as Bolan reached the house and ducked into the seven-foot-high hedgerow lining the front of the house, he began to wonder if he might be walking into a trap after all. Well, he couldn't worry about it in either case. Sandra Newbury's suffering and uncertain fate might have dictated action on Bolan's part.

But it was the Executioner who set the terms.

PERCY JETER LOOKED UP from his desk at the sound of a rap on the door frame of his massive office.

He recognized the head of his operations, Gabriel Mixon, who swept into the room. He was tall and muscular, and he wore his dark hair Marine Corps style: high and tight. Mixon carried the air of a soldier's soldier. They U.S. Navy had bounced him out of Basic Underwater Demolition School for beating one of his training candidates nearly to death. The general court-martial decided to conduct him out of the service with a Bad Conduct

Discharge—a term Mixon referred to as a Big Chicken Dinner—rather than imprisonment because the defense demonstrated the candidate had significantly provoked Mixon to violence.

Mixon couldn't stay out of trouble even once he left the Navy. His parents, ecologists for Greenpeace and secret supporters of a more radical faction of the ELF, had always supported protecting the environment by whatever means possible. Their views had ultimately gotten them killed. When they tried to commit a firebombing inside a university classroom where nuclear physics students were meeting, the police and EPA were waiting for them. A gun battle ensued that caused the premature explosion of the IED they were carrying, resulting in their deaths along with injury to six others in their group. The Feds hadn't suffered a single casualty in the incident. Fueled by rage and hatred, Mixon turned to a career in soldiering for any and every radical environmental protection group he could find. He became almost legendary in the ecoterrorist community for his ingenious choice of targets and his brutality.

"Looks like you were right, sir," Mixon said.

"About?"

"We just received a perimeter alarm from one of our hidden sentries. It looks like this Matt Cooper's trying to get inside the house."

"He's probably after the woman," Jeter replied. "Get Kellogg down here on the double. And for pity's sake, whatever you do don't let that Cooper maniac gain access to this house."

"Yes, sir." Mixon wheeled and left the room.

Great, that's all he needed right now. That son of a bitch Cooper was becoming a real thorn in Jeter's side. Why the hell couldn't he have stayed in Timber Vale where they could deal with him more effectively? Well, Jeter wasn't going to worry about it too much. Mixon had a competent team and there was no way Cooper could go up against forty trained ELF soldiers and survive. His encounter with the first hit team had been nothing more than pure luck; the team had obviously underestimated him. In fact, his sources said that they never had a chance, that Cooper had ambushed them with grenades and high explosives. And their second attempt didn't even qualify because they were nearly evenly numbered by Gowan's men and their cronies.

This time would be different, Jeter told himself.

Yes, today he would witness total victory!

18

It was so quiet—that Mack Bolan knew the enemy had detected his presence. Every sense screamed at him to get out of there. Bolan figured to leave now would only make matters worse, possibly even lead to the death of Sandra Newbury. She had stuck her neck out to bring down a bad cop, and Bolan owed her the military credo Leave No Man Behind.

Bolan found the front door to the house locked. He decided to look for a more opportune way inside, and found it in the form of a window left ajar on the north side of the château. The bottom ledge of the window was about two feet above his head, but Bolan scaled the obstacle by using the hand and foot grips of the flagstone facade. His feet now firmly on the ledge, Bolan eased the window open and looked into darkened interior, then ducked inside the opening and dropped gently to the floor. He closed the window and secured it behind him. Once more, it made no sense to alert a sentry on the off chance he still had the element of surprise on his side.

Bolan waited for his eyes to adjust to the gloom before crossing the room to a door on the other side. He cracked it wide enough to see it opened on to a grand central hallway with rooms on either side. A number of these probably served as guest quarters, although from the furniture scattered about the room Bolan figured he'd entered some kind of parlor. He opened the door wider, stuck his head out to look both ways and then stepped out and closed the door behind him.

No alarms sounded and no sentries rushed from alcoves or

shadows to challenge him. It was as if the place was deserted, and in that moment Bolan knew without a doubt that the enemy lay in wait. He'd been in too many situations like this before not to spot a trap. Bolan still had the element of surprise for them, though, because while they might be waiting for an opportune moment to pounce on him, they didn't know he expected them, and *that* he could use to his advantage.

Bolan continued along the wide hallway walking sideways with his back to the outside. In this way, he presented less of a target to any of the terrorists who might lie in wait for the right moment. It took a good tactician to spring a trap but a brilliant one to spring it at the right time, and Bolan had encountered very few brilliant ones through the years. Whoever served as chief strategist for the ELF proved to be no exception.

The challenge came at a moment when Bolan would have expected it most. As he reached the end of the hallway, a dozen or so terrorists entered through the front door at the opposite end of the château. The hallway at his end opened onto a broad room that sported a rug and pieces of heavy furniture arranged in a semicircle. Beyond that were stairs that split off from a central dais and rose in circular fashion to second-floor verandas that overlooked the area below. If the enemy had taken its time and put men in position directly above Bolan before launching their offense, he would have found himself pinned between them and the assault crew coming through the front door. Instead they had given him an evasion route to high ground and plenty of cover.

Bolan took advantage of the blunder and assumed a firing position on one knee behind a burgundy leather sofa. He brought the HK53 into battery, leveled it at the oncoming terrorists and triggered a pair of short bursts. The weapon bucked in his grasp, and flame spit from the muzzle as Bolan dispatched the enemy with a resolve and accuracy that had first earned him the Executioner moniker. The terrorists obviously realized it wouldn't prove as easy to take down their prey as they had first thought, and most of them either grabbed doorjambs for cover or hit the floor hard.

Two of the terrorists were a moment too late. One took a 3-round volley of high-velocity slugs to the chest. The impact slammed him against the wall next to the front door and he slid to the ground, a gory streak on the wall marking his journey. Another terrorist caught a round beneath the left eye. The pressure caused a periorbital blowout of the terrorist's eye socket and fractured his skull. His body spun and slammed into the wall, and he fell stiffly onto his back.

Bolan drilled a third terrorist with a volley to the gut that exited out his back. The man dropped his weapon in shock and looked down to see blood spurting from his midsection. Some of his entrails protruded visibly from between his fingers as he grabbed at his shredded stomach. He fell a moment later, first to his knees and then totally prone, most likely dead before his face hit the polished wooden floor.

SANDRA NEWBURY AWOKE to the sound of gunfire.

At first she thought maybe she had imagined it but then she heard it again, the clear and distinct rattle of autofire that could only come from assault weapons. A surge of hope went through her chilled, weary body, and she didn't doubt for a second Matt Cooper was the source of the ruckus above her head. She'd heard only silence to that point, but now there were the footfalls of running people above her, shouted commands and the unmistakable staccato of gunfire from a variety of automatic weapons.

Newbury looked furiously along the floor again in search of something she could use to break her bonds, but all she saw was dust and dirt. Damn it all! She thought about what else she might use to break free. She had nothing to counter the metal, which left only the thick leather of her manacles. Newbury considered using her teeth to gnaw at the tough leather but dismissed the idea as ludicrous. No way could her jaw withstand that kind of work.

Newbury shifted her position on the concrete slab and felt something stab her left buttock. She emitted a slight yelp and reached back to see what she'd sat on. A piece of the thin mat provided by her captors had been worn through by a sharp protrusion from the concrete slab. Not large but sufficient to wear through a seldom-used vinyl mat. Newbury smiled at her good fortune and repositioned her body at the other end of the slab.

With renewed vigor, Sandra Newbury began to use her legs to rub the leather straps against the sharp stone.

"WHAT THE HELL'S GOING ON?" Kellogg demanded as he entered Jeter's office under escort by Gabriel Mixon.

"What's going on?" Jeter reiterated. "Let me show you what's going on."

Jeter turned in his seat and pointed a remote at one of the bookshelves behind his desk. The unit slid aside to reveal a dozen or so LCD monitors that displayed various points of view of rooms throughout the château. Three of them showed the major firefight under way between Cooper and an ELF commando unit.

"Our friend Cooper there is making mincemeat out of my people!" Jeter's voice had taken on a dangerous tone. "That son of a bitch had the audacity to come here. Here where you said he wouldn't. You swore up and down he didn't know anything about our headquarters."

"He didn't!" Kellogg spit. "I sure as hell didn't tell him."

"Than why the fuck is he here, Jefferson? Eh?" Jeter lowered his voice. "Members of the Committee are supposed to start arriving within the hour. You had best hope he doesn't succeed in whatever he's come here to do, or you'll have *them* to answer to."

Kellogg started to say something, then leaned toward one of the monitors that displayed a picture of the ELF's makeshift dungeon. The picture seemed hazier and more opaque than the others, probably attributable to the poor lighting in that area, but Kellogg could make out enough of the picture to see Newbury working busily at the restraints on her feet.

"What the hell is she doing?" he asked. He turned and started for the door, "She's up to something. I'm going to get her out of there before Cooper gets to her."

"No, you're not," Jeter said. He reached into his desk drawer and withdrew a 9 mm pistol. "You're going to stay right here. Gabriel, relieve Mr. Kellogg of his sidearm."

Mixon nodded and stepped toward Kellogg. The FBI agent crouched, prepared to put up a fight, but Mixon had significantly more training and experience than Kellogg. He lashed out with an inside heel kick that caught Kellogg on the inner thigh just above the knee. The painful but nondebilitating kick distracted Kellogg. Mixon followed with a haymaker to the jaw. It fractured under the punch with an audible crack and knocked Kellogg to the floor. Mixon reached down, removed Kellogg's weapon from beneath his coat, then dumped him in a chair.

Kellogg held his knee and stared venomously at Mixon, who handed the pistol to Jeter.

"Thank you, Gabriel," Jeter said with a smile. "And now if you would be so kind as to go take care of Agent Newbury, we will wait here."

Mixon nodded, turned and smiled a death's-head smile at Kellogg, then exited the room.

Through clenched teeth, Kellogg said, "We had a deal, Jeter, you fucking traitorous rat. You promised I could walk out of here with my money. You gave me your word you'd pay me and that I could be on my way. What's a man without his word?"

"I'm terribly sorry if I disappointed you, Jefferson," Jeter said in a mocking tone of remorse. "But your bringing Cooper here has changed everything. Oh, we were expecting him to show up, of course, but his arrival has put our organization to considerable expense and disadvantage, and I'm afraid we're going to need the money we were paying you for the recruitment and training of personnel to replace the ones that he's downstairs killing right now!"

MACK BOLAN YANKED the magazine from the well of the HK53, flipped it over and inserted the second and final one as he ascended the stairs. Still a half dozen terrorists pursued him, moving down the hallway to the open foyer with caution. None of them were obviously so fanatical they gave no thought to self-preservation, uncaring if they wound up like their deceased comrades. As he reached the top of the stairs, Bolan released the slide catch and chambered a 5.56 mm round.

The warrior sprayed a short burst into the area below to keep heads down, then moved out of sight and kicked in the first door he came to. He shoulder-rolled into the room and came up on one knee. He swept the room with the HK53 muzzle but found no challengers. It was a bedroom, quiet and empty. Bolan left the room, cognizant of the sound of boots slapping the carpeted stairwell. He knew he couldn't possibly conduct a room-by-room search with the enemy hot on his heels and the likelihood that reinforcements would arrive any minute. There had to be another way; somebody had to know where they had imprisoned Newbury.

Bolan considered his options as the hesitant but steady sound of approaching terrorists drew nearer. A window at the end of the hallway drew his attention and an idea came to him. Bolan rushed to the next door and kicked it open, then the next and the next until he'd covered them all. He then rushed to the window, opened it and looked out to see the sill opened onto a ledge about a foot wide running the length of the château. The Executioner looked back to make sure no one had observed him, then jumped onto the ledge and closed the window behind him so that it barely latched. He crouched and waited patiently. If his idea panned out, the terrorists would reach the second floor and see the doors to every room open, confident that Bolan had already searched them. They would then continue through the hallway, which circled the outside of the entire second floor, and leave one or two sentries posted in that hallway in the event Bolan doubled back and they missed him.

A deathly quiet reigned outside. There were no sounds except for those of the chirp of a few birds. Bolan waited, breathed deeply and steadily to reduce the tension in his body and control the flow of adrenaline. A minute elapsed, then a second, and finally he heard voices draw nearer to the window. Bolan tensed his muscles, ready to respond if the enemy saw through his charade. He could make out the cast of human shadows over the window, as it was actually brighter inside the massive house.

The voices faded, and Bolan waited another minute before edging to the window and widening the crack ever so slightly. He looked in every direction, gradually easing the window open until he spotted what he was looking for. Sure enough, they had left a pair of sentries behind to deal with Bolan if he returned to that area.

The Executioner opened the window enough to climb onto the sill. The pair talked quietly, their backs to him, watching the entire length of the hallway. Bolan moved quietly into position, crouched and tensed his legs for the jump, then vaulted from the ledge toward the unaware sentries. He hit the pair full force, the impact knocking them to the ground. Bolan landed catlike on his feet and pounced on the first man like a cheetah on its prey. He drove a rock-hard fist into the back of the sentry's neck, jarring the spinal column and the base of the brain. The blow knocked the man senseless, and he slumped back to the floor unconscious.

The second sentry managed to get to his knees before Bolan cleared his Beretta from shoulder leather and then snaked a forearm around the sentry's neck. He yanked backward to take the terrorist off balance. Bolan held the guy in a viselike grip, the muscles of his forearm positioned just so that he could choke off air with a mere clenching of his fist.

He pressed the muzzle of the Beretta against the guy's ear. "Don't struggle and don't speak. The woman, the FBI agent Kellogg brought here. You know where she's being kept?"

The guy emitted a small grunt and a nod but didn't open his mouth.

"Good. Is she upstairs?"

A shake of the head.

"Where?"

The guy gestured downstairs.

Bolan considered this a moment and then decided the man was probably telling him the truth. He hadn't cleared every room on the first floor under the assumption the terrorists wouldn't have kept Newbury where she would be easily accessible by a rescue party. They would want her where they could get to her easily, though, and still make it difficult for Bolan to find her. At that moment the Executioner realized the terrorist didn't mean the first floor but a basement.

Bolan let off the pressure only slightly and then hauled the sentry to his feet. He nudged the muzzle against the back of the man's neck and ordered, "Lead on."

The pair traversed the hallway and took the stairs to the first floor. As they descended, two more sentries who had been left in the massive sitting room turned their faces in their direction. Bolan took each with a single subsonic round to the head, the Beretta 93-R generating a mere cough. It seemed unlikely the brief encounter would expose their position. The sound of men's voices moving above echoed down the stairs as the terrorists continued their futile search for Bolan.

The sentry led the Executioner to an alcove off the main living area and stopped at a heavy wooden door. Bolan gestured for him to open it and as soon as he did Bolan clipped the sentry behind the ear with the butt of his weapon. The terrorist guard dropped like a stone. The door swung open farther to reveal a small room with another metal door. Bolan dragged the guard inside, closed the door and then went to the inner door and tugged on the long, narrow handle. The door gave roughly with the creak of metal on concrete. Bolan stuck his head into the gloom beyond the open door, and the smell of musty, dank air tickled his senses. He took a cautious step inside and realized the floor gave way to a wooden staircase descending into a deep basement.

"Cooper?" a faint voice cracked.

"It's me," Bolan said.

"Finally," Sandra Newbury said, her voice stronger this time. "What the hell took you so long?"

"Later," Bolan said. He started down the steps and then realized he could get them both trapped below if they were discovered. He thought a moment, went back into the anteroom and searched the unconscious guard until he found a knife. Bolan went to the door and inspected the handle, then inserted the blade inside the catch and broke it off. Now the door wouldn't latch even if someone closed it on them.

Bolan darted down the steps. "You hurt?"

"No, just very tired." When he drew near she punched him the shoulder. "What the hell took you so long?" she repeated.

As he pulled the Ka-bar from his belt and began to cut through the leather—careful not to cut her foot with the razor-sharp blade as he inserted it between her skin and her bonds—he replied, "I was pacing myself. Right now, I'm going to need your help."

He'd just started to cut her free when sounds above commanded their attention.

19

A lone man, tall and muscular and dressed in a blacksuit not unlike Bolan's, stood at the top landing. The light from the anteroom glinted off the pistol he pointed steadily at them.

"Welcome, Mr. Cooper. I've been anxiously waiting for you to arrive." He kept the weapon trained on the couple as he started down the stairway.

"I'm sure," Bolan replied.

He stepped in front of Newbury and surreptitiously withdrew the Desert Eagle from its holster before passing it behind him. Newbury obviously noticed his movement because she immediately relieved him of it. Bolan had counted on the darkness to cover the subtle exchange, since the terrorist's eyes would not yet have adjusted to the gloom. He called it right because the man showed no sign he'd noticed the handoff.

"I assume you're in charge of this little outfit?"

"You could say that," the man replied. "The name's Gabriel Mixon. I'm captain of this training unit."

Bolan's eyes narrowed. "I know who you are. You've built quite a reputation as an ecoterrorist."

"I'm famous?"

Bolan laughed frostily. "Hardly. Unless you count famous as being on the most-wanted list of about a half-dozen countries."

"Be careful, Cooper," Mixon said. "I wouldn't want that kind of thing to get out to my benefactors. They don't like anything to draw attention to operations."

"I don't really care. After today, your operations are through."

Mixon reached the bottom of the steps, but he didn't get closer. Bolan couldn't be sure if Newbury could get off a clear shot from where she sat. It made him feel helpless but if he didn't think Newbury could handle it, Bolan would have never given her the pistol. Sometimes there were moments when a soldier had to entrust his life to the hands of another. It wasn't easy but it was fact.

"I think you're mistaken, Cooper. In fact our operations are just getting started. The attack on Kingsley Airfield was only the beginning."

"You're the one who's mistaken," Bolan shot back. "Within an hour this place will be swarming with police and Army National Guard. The ELF is finished."

"I don't think so," Mixon said with a snicker. "You see, I've come to learn a lot about how you operate. I don't know who are you, Cooper, but if I've learned anything it's that you're like me."

It was Newbury's turn to deliver a derisive retort. "He's nothing like you, shit-head."

Mixon stared hard at her a moment and then said, "I meant that he likes to operate alone. And it's that preference that leads me to believe he hasn't called upon any reinforcements. I wondered why he would risk coming here at all, why he wouldn't just locate us and call in heavy guns, and then it occurred to me. He would want to attempt a rescue, try to pull this poor, defenseless woman from our evil clutches before she came to harm. Isn't it touching?"

"Well, the joke's on you, Mixon," Bolan said. "I figured this might be some kind of trap."

"Nothing quite so sinister, Cooper. I was sent down to take care of your girlfriend here. You're just the bonus." Mixon actually laughed and then took a couple of steps toward them. "I think I'll let her watch you die first."

The Executioner had expected the report of the Desert Eagle, so he didn't even flinch at the discharge. It practically deafened him, and he felt the heat from the muzzle-flash given the proximity of the weapon when Newbury fired. The 300-grain boattail slug caught Mixon square in the center of his chest. The pistol flew from his fingers as the impact drove him off his feet. The back of his head smacked the concrete wall with a sickly splat, and he crumpled into a lifeless heap at the base of the steps.

"What took you so long?" Bolan asked.

Newbury smiled as she lowered the smoking muzzle of the .44 Magnum pistol and replied, "I was pacing myself."

There was the sound of renewed activity above their heads.

"That's our cue," Bolan said as he quickly traded Newbury the Beretta for his Desert Eagle and then finished sawing through her bonds with the Ka-bar.

As they ascended the steps, Newbury asked, "You have a plan for getting out of here?"

"Yeah, but there's still one little detail I need to deal with."

"What's that?"

"Kellogg," the Executioner replied.

JETER WATCHED THE SCENE in the basement unfold in utter helplessness. He hadn't seen the exchange between Cooper and Newbury, nor could he have done anything about it if he had. A tinge of guilt and remorse clutched Jeter's chest as he watched Mixon gunned down ruthlessly in front of his eyes, then watched as Cooper freed Newbury and the two of them escaped. There would be no stopping them now. The best he could hope for was that his people held Cooper off long enough for his chopper to arrive. Jeter looked at the clock and realized the chairman of the Committee would arrive within the next fifteen minutes.

"Looks like this didn't turn out the way you expected after all, Percy," Kellogg taunted.

Jeter had to admit that Kellogg was right. This Matt Cooper had possibly destroyed any chance he had of earning his seat on the Committee. The others on the Committee would never confirm his nomination as a member unless he could somehow turn this around to his advantage. Maybe he could find another location to continue operations, gather the remnants of his team for a new operation against Timber Vale.

"He'll come for you next, you know," Kellogg continued with a sneer.

Jeter jumped from his chair, whirled and pointed the pistol at Kellogg's head. "Shut up, you little fuck! I'm tired of you and your pathetic whining. You're nothing but a miserable sloth, an insignificant insect."

"Go ahead and kill me, then, Percy," Kellogg challenged. "Go ahead and pull the trigger and take away your only chance of getting out of here alive."

Jeter hesitated. "What are you talking about?"

"You think I'd come in here without a way out? You think I'm stupid?"

"I think you're lying."

"You willing to take that chance?" Kellogg demanded. "Listen to me and listen close, Percy. You don't stand a chance against Cooper alone. You aren't trained for this kind of thing. Mixon's dead, and I'm willing to let your little betrayal go. Think about it, Percy…I'm all you have left!"

Jeter didn't want to admit it, but he knew Kellogg spoke the truth. He stood little chance of escaping in the helicopter before Cooper got to him. Their unit hadn't been able to stop him before, and there was even less chance they would now that Newbury was free and Mixon dead. Not to mention the fact that the police and rangers were probably on their way right at that moment.

"All right, Jefferson," Jeter conceded. "But you better not be screwing me here or I swear I'll make sure I kill you. You hear me?"

Kellogg nodded quickly and then got to his feet. "Can I have my gun back?"

Jeter squinted at him with an expression of disbelief, and Kellogg let it drop. He turned and gestured for Jeter to follow. Jeter kept a reasonable distance between them as they left the third-story office and descended the steps. He wondered what sort of transportation Kellogg had arranged for, but he didn't think it was important to spend time chitchatting about it. Probably the guy had a four-wheeler or motorcycle stashed. Once Kellogg showed Jeter where he'd hidden the transportation, he'd kill the Fed and strike out on his own. He could always get to a nearby city and make more suitable arrangements from there.

As they got closer to the first floor, the sounds of battle grew more intense.

BOLAN AND NEWBURY MADE the first floor and relieved the fallen sentries of their SMGs. Most of the ELF terrorists were carrying MP-5s but a few—and one of the pair in this case—had a Steyr MPi 69. Bolan gave Newbury the MP-5, confident she would feel much less awkward with it than the Steyr. Most agents were required to undergo antiterrorist training courses during their time at the FLETC. This included hands-on instruction, as well as drills using both M-16 carbines and MP-5s.

Bolan and Newbury took up covering positions on either side of the hallway as a half-dozen terrorists descended the steps from the second floor. Bolan would have preferred to have the high ground, but at least surprise was on their side. The terrorists came into view. Bolan held up his hand to signal they should hold fire until they had better line of sight. Thankfully, Newbury followed the Executioner's lead.

Bolan cut his hand through the air, and the pair opened up on their enemies. The first two terrorists fell under Bolan's marksmanship. The MPi 69 chattered in his fists, and a hailstorm of 9 mm slugs scythed through the two terrorists leading the descending charge. Blood sprayed in all directions as they continued down the steps, tumbling now.

The sight of their deceased comrades bouncing and rolling down the steps distracted the remaining terrorists. It was clear to Bolan that the vast majority of the ELF's troops weren't accustomed to facing an enemy who fought back. They were terrorists, and as such they weren't trained to react defensively when encountering trained combatants like Bolan and Newbury. That proved a weak spot, and Bolan filed it away for future reference.

Newbury neutralized the other four terrorists with impressive accuracy and efficiency. One took a full burst to the chest that slammed the terrorist against the wall. Two more fell with large holes punched through their chest, and the final one took a shot to the skull that blew his head apart. The terrorist's body stiffened and then seemed to fall forward in slow motion. It landed on the steps with a dull thud as the echo of gunfire died away.

"Clear?" Newbury shouted out of pure reflex and training.

"Clear," Bolan answered.

The Executioner got to his feet and rushed to her position. "You need to get out of here."

"What about you?" she asked.

"I told you there's still some unfinished business with Kellogg."

"Kellogg's my problem," she said. "As long as he's alive, it's my duty to make sure he's apprehended. He betrayed a lot of good people and the badge, and I plan to do everything I can to make sure he stands before a judge and jury to answer for it."

"He will, believe me," Bolan countered. "But this is my show, and you need to be around to gather the evidence against him."

Newbury eyed him a moment longer and said, "Promise me you'll take him alive."

"Sandra, I can't—"

"Promise me!" she demanded. "Or I'm not going anywhere!"

"Okay," Bolan said. "I'll do everything I can to take him alive."

Newbury nodded and then rose, turned on her heel and headed for the exit.

DON CLINT SAT on the ridge and watched helplessly as the drama below unfolded.

Through the binoculars he observed Cooper's approach, watched him get past the security system and finally make it to the house. But then it all went to hell in a handbasket when just shortly after Cooper made his entry a gaggle of armed men rushed from the woods and headed for the château. For a long while Clint did nothing. He'd given Cooper his word to wait right there and be ready to provide covering fire when Cooper came out and gave the signal.

From a distance he heard the reports of automatic weapons coming from within the house. At times the noise would wane and then start again, but eventually it ceased altogether. And then Clint observed Cooper climb out a window and wait on a ledge running along the second floor and a warm glow renewed his spirit as he realized Cooper had the situation well in hand. More time passed and Clint kept checking his watch.

Finally, he could bear it no longer. He knew he should keep his promise, but he couldn't stand idly by while a good man like Cooper fell under the teeth of crooked federal cops and ecoterrorist jackals. If this was his day of reckoning, then Clint wanted that day to be on his terms.

Clint made his descent from the obscure promontory in record time for a man his age. He reached the edge of the woods and crouched in a clump of tall wheat grass. Directly ahead, about thirty yards or so, sat the small outbuilding Cooper had identified as containing security equipment. Clint watched the surroundings for several minutes but detected no movement. He came to a decision, rose and trotted in a half crouch to the door of the outbuilding. He reached down and tried the handle. It turned easily, and Clint first pushed and then pulled to determine the direction of the door's movement. To his disappointment, it opened outwardly—that would make taking any occupants by surprise a tad more difficult.

Clint counted to three and then ripped the door open and charged inside. A man sat in a chair monitoring a series of camera displays and control panels. What a dumb puppy this one, Clint thought, sitting with his back to the door. Before the guy could react Clint smacked him in the back of the head with the butt of his .308 rifle. The guy emitted a groan and slumped forward in his chair. Clint reached out, grasped the back of the man's collar and hauled his unconscious form out of the chair.

Then he jacked the lever of the rifle and murmured, "Time to even things up a bit."

AS THEY MADE THEIR ESCAPE with Jeter's gun at his back, Kellogg cursed himself for his indiscretion when it came to choosing allies. Though he'd never liked Percy Jeter, he thought that between the Gowan crime Family and the ELF the latter would be the lesser of two evils. Obviously he'd misjudged Jeter and what amounted to little more than a group of incompetent, disorganized, tree-hugging thugs. In just a short time Cooper had managed to take down an enterprise that all the resources of the nation's law-enforcement agencies and the Gowan underworld had been unable to do. He admitted a modicum of respect for anybody like that.

Kellogg considered his options. He might find a moment where Jeter let his guard down long enough to disarm him, but what then? He could try making it out on foot but the weather hadn't been that cooperative so far, and if he didn't reach some point of civilization before dark he could either wander around aimlessly until he fell off a cliff or froze to death. Neither scenario held much appeal for him so he decided to play along. He didn't actually have any alternate mode of transport away from there. He'd blurted it out in the heat of the moment, a desperate if not simply pathetic way of saving his own life. At best, he'd probably done little more than delay his untimely demise.

As they reached the second floor, they encountered a small battery of ELF troops cloistered around their squad leader.

"What's going on?" Jeter demanded.

"We're waiting for orders from Captain Mixon," the squad leader sputtered.

"Mixon's dead," Jeter snapped. "You're in charge now. I want you to set up a perimeter and then find the intruders and kill them. I'll also need a couple of your men to escort us to some escape vehicles we have waiting outside. Once you've neutralized the enemy, you'll need to maintain a perimeter and wait for members of the Committee to arrive."

"Understood, sir." The squad leader gestured to two of his people, one male and one female, with instructions to accompany Jeter and Kellogg.

Well, that effectively did away with any remote chance of overpowering Jeter. Kellogg considered all other options and decided if he were going to make his play, it had to be…

Now! The rogue FBI agent edged closer to the female who stood with her SMG held casually in her hands, muzzle pointed toward the floor. Within a second he had his hands wrapped around hers, pivoted on the soles of his feet and executed a perfect Judo throw that sent the woman tumbling into Jeter and the squad leader. Weapon in hand, Kellogg turned the weapon on the four ELF crew members still standing and depressed the trigger in a sustained burst as he swept the area in a corkscrew pattern. Warm blood splattered onto his clothes and walls around him given the closeness of the MP-5. The 9 mm slugs ripped through vital organs and scattered the ELF terrorists in every direction. Kellogg let out a blood-curdling scream as he cut a deadly swath of bullets through the close-in group before a single one could bring a weapon to bear.

Kellogg stopped firing long enough to track the MP-5 on Jeter and the remaining pair of terrorists still trying to disentangle from each other. He depressed the trigger once more, a short burst this time that blew four neat holes in the squad leader's chest. He then stepped forward and kicked the woman terrorist in the back of the head. The blow smashed her face into the floor. Kellogg had enough self-pride that he wasn't going to simply shoot a defenseless female in the back.

The smoking muzzle of the MP-5 now came to rest mere inches from Percy Jeter's face. The ELF terror leader looked for the pistol that had been knocked from his grasp, but it had skittered across the polished hardwood floor and come to a stop well out of his reach. Jeter stared past the muzzle to look Kellogg in the eyes, his expression a mask of pure hate.

Kellogg smiled. "Well, Percy, it seems fortunes have changed. I told you not to try fucking me over."

"Go ahead and do whatever you're going to do," Jeter replied.

"Gladly," Kellogg said as he squeezed the trigger.

20

After verifying Newbury's safe departure from the building, Bolan began a hard probe for Kellogg. He had to admit the size of the ELF force had thrown him for a loop. He hadn't realized their assault crews probably qualified as nothing short of a small army—Bolan estimated more than thirty—and it told him they had to have been planning a substantial operation against Timber Vale. That head count didn't even include the special-assault units he'd encountered at the mill and the hotel.

A pair of ELF terrorists tried to ambush him on the stairs, but the Executioner was prepared for such eventualities. In their haste to destroy him they hadn't noticed the Russian-made hand grenade Bolan had procured from one of the deceased terrorists, and while they were busy trying to cut him down with autofire they failed to see the grenade bounce between them just a moment before it exploded. The high explosive rocked the second-floor landing with enough shock and heat to separate limbs from the pair of terrorists. Plaster and charred wood rained on Bolan as he charged up the steps and past the grisly corpses.

A trio of terrorists appeared at the far end of the hallway and took up firing positions along the sides of the corridor. Bolan knelt and triggered a short burst that caught one terrorist in the shoulder and spun her into a door. She dropped her weapon and let out a scream, but Bolan had already sighted on his next target. A sustained maelstrom of rounds buzzed past Bolan's head before he could gather a decent bead on his target. Something in his gut screamed for Bolan to roll, and he followed the instinct in time to take a graze in the left hip that would have struck him in the abdomen had he not moved.

Bolan finished his roll in a prone position and with a much better vantage point than before. He triggered the MPi 69 and a fusillade of rounds hammered another terrorist center mass. The 9 mm slugs punched through the man's chest and stomach and flipped him onto his back.

The macabre sight combined with the screaming female seemed to cause a psychological impairment on the remaining gunman, because the rounds he fired at Bolan went high and wide. The Executioner exploited the advantage and felled the terrorist with a 3-round burst to the head. The man's skull exploded, and the headless corpse crumpled to the floor.

Bolan rose and charged toward the female terrorist trying to reach for her weapon with her wounded shoulder while covering the wound with her palm. Bolan arrived in time to kick the weapon out of her grasp. He almost continued past her and then stopped, thought better of it and knelt by her side. Bolan pulled her hand away and a fresh torrent of blood began to seep from the wound.

"Looks like the clavicle vein's been hit," Bolan said.

He looked into her eyes. She tried to maintain a haughty appearance, but behind the tough mask Bolan could see a deep and overriding desire to break into tears. Obviously she'd never been shot before and it was likely she'd never killed anyone before, either. Bolan wasn't naive enough to think that made the young woman less dangerous but he could hardly hold it against her. Bolan guessed she was no older than nineteen or twenty, and she certainly hadn't spent much time in the terrorist game.

"Just leave me alone," she whispered between clenched teeth.

"If I leave you alone you'll bleed to death, sister," Bolan snapped. The soldier reached to the combat med pouch on his belt and withdrew the only bulky compress dressing he had. He pressed it against her shoulder and then gently grabbed her hand and instructed her to hold it there while he tied off a knot on her neck designed to staunch the flow of blood.

"Why are you helping me?" she asked as he worked.

"Because I'm not a beast," Bolan replied. "That's one of the things that separate civilized human beings from wild animals. Compassion."

"You mean the same animals our government has poisoned with its technology and industry?" she spit.

"I don't have time to argue ecological philosophy, lady," Bolan countered sternly. He finished the work and pinned her with an ice-blue stare. "But I've got news for you—the U.S. government's not the culprit here. It's greedy industrialists and organized crime lords who've been financing your little operation. The very people you're working for are the ones who do the least to help our environment. You might think about that when they ask you to testify to save your own neck."

Bolan whipped a set of plastic rigo cuffs from the cargo pocket of his woodland-camouflage coveralls and secured the wrist of her uninjured arm to the hinge of the door she leaned against. He then rose and continued his search for Kellogg, leaving the totally stupefied young woman sitting there to stew with her mouth agape.

SANDRA NEWBURY CLEARED the château's front door but didn't reach the end of the covered porch before a crew of terrorists opened up on her position. Newbury reacted with all the dictates of her training, grabbing cover behind a thick support post amid the hedgerows bordering the house with a speed and agility born from an uncompromising regimen of physical conditioning.

Back to the thick post, Newbury brought her knees to her chest with the MP-5 held muzzle pointing skyward as a maelstrom of rounds zinged into the bushes on either side of her. More rounds hammered the wood post, and Newbury could hear and feel every single one of them as they vibrated with the impact. It wouldn't take long for the shooters to transform that post to a toothpick if they maintained that kind of suppressive fire. Every few seconds she would hear one or two of the weapons drop out of the full and ceaseless chatter while the shooters changed out magazines, but then they would rejoin the furious fusillade.

Newbury didn't see how she could risk moving from her position without a lull in the firing. The terrorists kept up the barrage for nearly a full minute and then out of the steady buzz of reports Newbury heard the clear crack of a high-powered rifle resound through the chill air. The autofire suddenly seemed to lessen and with the report of a second and third rifle shot Newbury noticed a definite drop in the assault.

Newbury waited a moment longer, and the bullets that had been whizzing around her ceased. The autofire had changed direction now, and the enemy no longer seemed interested in firing on her. Newbury counted to five, took a deep breath and burst from cover. She charged out of the bushes and headed away from the general direction of the fire. Newbury spotted a long, low outbuilding, maybe thirty yards in width, and charged it with renewed hope. The dirt at her feet erupted as at least one shooter tried to take her down, but Newbury made the cover of the building before a single round found its mark. Newbury circled to the front of the building and charged through a door, weapon held at the ready. Only silence and a horrific smell opposed her. To her surprise she had stormed a communal outhouse.

Newbury kept low and rushed to a window that would afford her a view of the general area where she suspected the terrorists were hiding. A few muzzle-flashes along the eastern wood line betrayed their position. From the window of another outbuilding Newbury saw muzzle-flashes as three more rifle shots rang out. The FBI agent didn't know who her guardian angel was—other than it couldn't possibly have been Cooper—but she did know it was time to return the favor. Newbury snapped open the screened window, leveled the foregrip of her MP-5 on the window ledge and triggered a sustained burst into the wood line. Dirt and leaves marked where her rounds struck, and Newbury corrected her line of fire on the fly. The rifle contributed to the onslaught by narrowing the time between shots—the marksman had stepped up his game.

Newbury kept it up until the bolt slammed back on an empty chamber, and then she changed out magazines and sent more rounds into the woods, this time in more controlled bursts targeted just behind the muzzle-flashes. When she'd emptied that magazine, as well, Newbury tossed the spent MP-5 aside and withdrew the Beretta from her waistband. She steadied her hands on the windowsill and waited, watched for movement in the tall grass or looked for a muzzle-flash or reflection of light on metal. Once in a while her eyes would flick toward the other outbuilding but she saw no movement, no more muzzle-flashes, nothing.

Newbury's heartbeat slowed, and eventually she couldn't hear the rush of blood in her ears. She concentrated every sense on the woods but no threat presented itself. Newbury knew that any surviving terrorists could play this waiting game for a long time. Another few minutes elapsed, although it seemed like an eternity, and then movement in Newbury's peripheral vision demanded her attention. A man emerged from the door of the small outbuilding. He wasn't overly tall, and from that distance his gait suggested he wasn't that young, either. He walked carefully but steadily toward the wood line.

He's out of his mind!

Newbury watched as the man approached the tall grassy area where just a few minutes before a half-dozen terrorists or more had been shooting at them. She kept the Beretta trained on those swaying grasses, ignoring the cold air that bit through the thin material of her blouse. She'd left her jacket in her car where it obviously stayed after her encounter with Kellogg and the ELF goons. Newbury pushed the cold and discomfort from her mind, focusing her sights on the enemy's front lines, ready to rejoin the battle if necessary.

Eventually the rifleman disappeared into the shadows of the wood line. Newbury waited, concentrated on breathing slow and steady. A few minutes passed and then the man reappeared, removed the fur hat from his head and waved it high in the air while looking in her direction. She couldn't hear what he was shouting, but she understood the all-clear signal. Newbury turned and left the outhouse. She kept her pistol held at the ready as she walked toward where the man stood. His features became distinct as she drew clearer and she realized he was even older than she expected.

When she was within ten yards she stopped.

"Hi," he said with a grin. "I'm guessing you're Sandra."

She cocked her head. "Yeah. And you are?"

He stepped forward and extended his hand. "Don Clint, U.S. Forestry officer, retired. I'm pleased to see you're alive."

"You came with Cooper?" she asked as she reached out to shake his hand. When he nodded, she quipped, "You're one of the lucky ones, then. He's not much for help."

"I'm afraid he didn't have much of a choice in this one," Clint replied.

The faint sound of an approaching helicopter intruded on their conversation.

"Given our recent experiences, we might want to find some cover for now," Clint suggested.

"Won't get any arguments from me," Newbury replied and the pair dashed for the nearby tree line.

JEFF KELLOGG WAITED at the base of the steps on the back side of the château. The steps descended from a rooftop egress and were concealed between an exterior wall and the frame wall of the house. They were only visible from directly above, which made them particularly convenient in the situation. Kellogg checked his weapon a couple of times and intermittently studied his watch. The helicopter should have been here by now! *What the hell was taking them so long?* he wondered.

Kellogg had already formed his plan. He'd wait until the occupants had cleared the helicopter, and then he would approach on the flank where the pilot couldn't see him. At least one of the passengers was a member of the Committee and would be accompanied by bodyguards, so if Kellogg had to take them out he'd want to do so without posing any hazards to the chopper.

That bird represented his only way out of here, and he didn't intend to let the opportunity slip through his fingers.

The best he could hope for would be that the ELF could hold off Cooper long enough to effect Kellogg's escape. Every so often he caught the sound of autofire, and even once he'd heard an explosion. Cooper was one dangerous son of a bitch, Kellogg thought, and the FBI agent wasn't too proud to admit his happiness at having never had to go against Cooper firsthand. The biggest challenge now would be getting to LAX and out of the country via the private jet he'd chartered before anybody got wise to his escape. Once he reached the Caymans he'd withdraw his cash, close his accounts and head for some remote village in South America where he could live out his existence in comfort. Maybe he would find a nice Brazilian beauty to settle down with and raise a few kids.

The sound of chopper blades slapping the air reached his ears and sent Kellogg's senses into high alert. At last his chariot had come. Kellogg tightened the grip on his MP-5 and tensed his legs. He kept his back pressed to the wall of the stairwell landing and listened with glee as the sound of freedom drew nearer by the moment. Soon the entire building shook with the vibration and a gust of wind twisted its way down the steps and brushed his hair lightly. He could sense the steady thrum of the rotors as they pulsed through the wall and caused his insides to rumble.

In just a few minutes, Jeff Kellogg would be airborne and on his way to freedom.

THE EXECUTIONER WATCHED through the edge of the blinds that covered the sliding glass patio doors. Beyond the expanse of decorative concrete was an Olympic-size ground-level pool, empty and covered for the winter. Bordering the patio and pool on the north side was the helipad. Bolan's search of the house did not uncover Kellogg, but it did reveal the bullet-riddled body of a man whose driver's license identified him as Percy Jeter.

Bolan knew the name well. Jeter stood as a figure of promi-

nence in Wonderland. He had a reputation for rubbing elbows in
many influential circles, especially those involved with charitable programs designed for developmentally disabled children.
Here was a guy who had turned his back on everything that was
important just so he could make a few extra bucks while chairing
a very socially conscientious and worthwhile effort, improving
the life of children with mental and physical disabilities. The
worst kind of vermin had been Percy Jeter, preying on the pocketbooks of the weak and helpless. He'd gotten exactly what he
deserved in the Executioner's book.

Bolan eventually located Jeter's office on the third-floor suite
and a few minutes poking through records was all it took for him
to discover Jeter had expected the arrival of a helicopter carrying
some VIPs. At that point, Bolan had taken the time to use Jeter's
phone and place a call to Stony Man. Kurtzman had advised him
on the impending arrival of the National Guard and federal law
enforcement in short order. He decided to wait downstairs for the
new arrivals.

The helicopter touched down and as its rotors slowed and the
whine of the engine faded, the Executioner stepped onto the
patio and headed toward the chopper while its passengers disembarked. Under normal circumstances, Bolan wouldn't have
looked the least bit out of place, and the group of several distinguished men in suits who climbed from the chopper didn't appear
alarmed to see an armed man in camouflage approach them.

The sudden emergence of Jeff Kellogg from an alcove caught
Bolan off guard, and this produced a tempestuous and equal
reaction from Kellogg as he locked eyes with the Executioner.
The men in suits became fearful as they exchanged glances with
both men. The two armed bodyguards escorting the team of dignitaries considered Kellogg the threat but didn't have time to
react before Kellogg cut them down with a sweep of the MP-5.

However, Kellogg's haste to eliminate any barriers between
him and the helicopter bought the Executioner the time he needed
to bring the .44 Magnum Desert Eagle to bear. Bolan snap-aimed

and squeezed the trigger twice. The first round hammered Kellogg's SMG, turning the weapon to junk metal and driving it from his fists. The second round contacted his right side and shattered the bone. The impact spun Kellogg and knocked him to the ground.

The VIPs were now prone on the concrete with their hands covering their heads. Bolan rushed the helicopter, the Desert Eagle trained on Kellogg's motionless form and the MPi 69 pointed toward the pilot. Bolan gestured with the weapon, indicating the pilot should step out. Once the man had vacated the helicopter and joined the others on the ground, Bolan felt for a pulse at Kellogg's neck. He found it.

Newbury and Clint joined Bolan less than a minute later, and Newbury looked at Kellogg before shooting the Executioner a hard stare.

Bolan grinned. "He's alive."

Newbury nodded at him with an expression of gratitude. "I'm impressed, Cooper. You kept your word. You must be getting soft in your old age."

"Could be," Bolan replied.

One of the VIPs on the ground looked up at them. "Just who the hell are you people?"

Don Clint exchanged glances with Bolan and Newbury, then toed the man lightly in the ribs and replied, "You got the right to remain silent, fella, so why don't you shut your yap?" Then he looked back at Bolan with a sigh. "You know, at times I sure do miss this stuff."

21

Mack Bolan met Mickey Gowan's Timber Vale operations with a full-on blitz. Thanks to some assistance from Stony Man, state police and federal agents swarmed the area and ran interference against the corrupt local law enforcement, as well as Chep Flannery's vigilante force.

With war averted between Gowan's hard cases and the town's citizens, the Executioner met Gowan's enforcement team on his own terms.

Bolan commandeered the ELF's chopper, and an Oregon Air National Guard pilot gladly volunteered to ferry the Executioner into Timber Vale. The pilot brought the chopper into a hover above the small, nondescript insurance building that a talkative Kellogg, trying to avoid additional prosecution, identified as the headquarters for Gowan's operation. Based on Bolan's description of the face he'd seen leaving the firefight of the motel, Kellogg identified Struthers Sullivan, Gowan's premier assassin and executive officer.

Fully geared in his blacksuit and armed to the teeth, Bolan descended to the roof of the insurance agency at just past midnight. The quartet of vehicles parked outside the building served as evidence that Gowan's entourage had arrived in Timber Vale. His thugs were inside planning violent deeds against the innocent bystanders and good, hard-working business owners.

Mack Bolan was going to see to it that plan never came to fruition.

The Executioner rappelled down the line and dropped gracefully onto the roof. He shoulder-rolled through the landing and came up on his feet, never losing momentum as he charged to the edge of the roof. Bolan wrapped the wire line of the chopper around a stanchion and then vaulted over the side of the building and arced through the wide front window. He slapped at the carabiner and dropped to a crouch.

Gowan's soldiers were clustered in the back of the office, gathered around a long table with papers strewed across it. Cigarette smoke drifted in the halo from a pair of bright lamps suspended from the ceiling. The group of thugs whirled at Bolan's dramatic entry, but the others were taken by complete surprise at the swift and violent assault.

One guy actually managed to clear hardware from leather before Bolan leveled his Colt Model R0639 SMG and triggered a short burst. A trio of 9 mm rounds ripped through the gunman's chest and slammed him against the wall with enough force that the back of his skull cracked the heavy wire-mesh glass of the rearmost office door.

Most of Gowan's goons dived to the floor, but a couple tried to flee and only ended up bumping into one another. Bolan brought the carbine-style weapon to his shoulder and squeezed the trigger twice more. The straight-line design followed that of the M-4 Carbine and Commando models, and it provided the quick, close-up capability Bolan knew he would need for the operation. The weapon chattered with the repeated triggering of 3-round bursts, adding to the noise and confusion of men shouting and scrambling over one another to find cover from the hailstorm of lead thrown at them. The two men who tumbled into each other died as slugs punctured their chests. One also caught a bullet to the throat and his hands reached to the bloody, raw wound as blood spurted from his mangled carotid arteries. The man died on his feet and his body toppled to the ground.

Bolan yanked a flash-bang grenade from his LBE, primed it and delivered the projectile in an easy overhand toss as he changed positions. He sought cover behind a support pillar, covered his ears, squeezed his eyes shut and opened his mouth wide. The lull in the firing prompted a couple of Gowan's soldiers to rise and return fire with their pistols, but ultimately the effort proved futile, since they were firing into an area Bolan no longer occupied. The flash-bang ignited a moment later, instantly blinding both men and rupturing the eardrums of several more.

Bolan broke cover, his Colt SMG held at the ready. Somebody managed to open the rear office door and scramble free on hands and knees. Bolan set off on a pursuit course and dispatched a pair of pistol-toting hoods who had somehow managed to escape the major-effects grenade. Bolan kept the SMG tight and low as he triggered a sweeping blast that cut splotchy red patterns across the midsection of both men. They collapsed into heaps and Bolan continued forward, stepping around the pile of dead or disabled hard cases.

The Executioner burst into the back room and immediately crouched. The instinctive move saved his life as the escapee burst from behind a desk and triggered two rounds that whizzed overhead close enough for Bolan to hear their passage. He recognized the shooter instantly as Struthers Sullivan. He leveled his weapon and squeezed the trigger. The 9 mm slugs struck Sully in the chest, entering the body with an upward trajectory, and punched through lung and heart tissue before exiting out the upper back. The impact sent Sully reeling into a filing cabinet with enough force to dent the thin, light gray metal drawers.

A look of horror mixed with surprise splashed across the man's face and froze there like a death mask as his lifeless body slid to the ground. He reached a sitting position and then, with a last gurgling cough of blood, Struthers Sullivan slumped onto his side and succumbed to death.

The sounds of battle died, and Bolan rose slowly amid the smoke of gunfire and smell of death. The air of violence and spent energies clung to the Executioner like a heavy cloak. All told the battle had taken less than a minute. But the threat had been quelled, and from that night forward the citizens of Timber

Vale could rest without fear of reprisal. Bolan had crushed the ELF's terror machine, and all that remained now was to topple the head of the Gowan underworld. And it was a task Mack Bolan relished.

MICKEY GOWAN LISTENED to the news in weighty silence, not interrupting or asking questions. When the caller finished his report, Gowan quietly thanked him and gently hung up the phone.

Gone.

All of his men, nearly every enforcer in his personal cadre, had been killed or captured by the police. With the exception of the house guards, which numbered only a half dozen, his entire enforcement crew had fallen to the brutality and murderous fervor of one man: Matt Cooper. Gowan could hardly find his voice. He wanted to call out to his men in anger, summon Sully and tell him to take his boys and find Cooper and turn the guy's world into blood and ashes. But that would never be now. The caller, whose voice Mickey didn't recognize, had told him the call was only being made out of respect and that he had personally seen the body of Struthers Sullivan carried from their operating headquarters in Timber Vale.

Gowan couldn't believe that Sully was gone, and yet somehow he knew it was true. The caller had also mentioned that he had nothing to worry about as far the ELF was concerned. Cooper had also apparently taken them down, and Kellogg had been captured.

"Word on the street has it he'll be turning state's evidence against you, Mickey," the caller said. "You might want to get out of town while you still can. In fact, you should probably head for Ireland."

Yeah, that's what he'd do. He could return to the motherland and hole up there until all of this blew over. After all, Mickey Gowan was respected back there, even worshipped in some circles, and they would protect him. He could live it up there, four or five years—he could also do some traveling abroad as long as they were in countries that denied U.S. extradition—then return to the U.S. when things had quieted some.

Gowan made up his mind and got out of bed. His wife stirred next to him, mumbled something he didn't hear and then turned over and went back to her snoring. She'd always slept heavy like that. Well, this time he wouldn't be taking her with him. He'd see to it she went some place safe, somewhere the Feds couldn't find her, and he'd return to Belfast and visit with friends. He slipped into his robe, rattling off a list of details under his breath he needed to attend, and then headed into the adjoining recreation room.

His hands shook as he pawed and clawed his way past several bottles until he found the expensive Irish whiskey he kept stashed there. Gowan drew it out and located a glass. He thought he heard a noise and froze in his tracks. The track lights along the far end provided the only illumination. Gowan's eyes came to rest on the large, oil-based portrait mounted beneath those lights. The hard green eyes of his father stared back at him—his father's stare had always created apprehension in him—and he averted his eyes.

Gowan slapped the wall switch for the lights above the wet bar, but nothing happened. He touched the sensors a few more times, a little harder with each touch, but still nothing happened. He muttered under his breath, tucked the glass under his arm and carried the whiskey and a small tub of ice over to a table near the picture of his father. Gowan sat on the sofa, dropped a few cubes into the glass and then filled it from the decanter.

Mickey Gowan sat back and took a large swallow from the glass. As the whiskey burned the back of his throat and brought a little water to his eyes, he looked into his father's eyes once more. Finally, after taking a few more drinks, he took the half-full glass and hurled it at the picture. The glass shattered against the fine oils and left an ugly smear where his father's chin had been.

Gowan felt the sensation of cold metal press against the back of his head and heard the unmistakable click of a pistol's action.

"Temper, temper," a hard voice said.

Gowan recognized that voice immediately. It was the same voice he'd heard over the telephone not five minutes before.

"Who are you?" Gowan said, his voice cracking. "Why don't you leave me alone? What have I ever done to you, wanker?"

"What you've done to all those innocent people, you've done to me," Mack Bolan replied. "There's no getting around that fact."

"What people?"

"Everyone you've ever cheated, robbed, murdered or exploited. Your porn shops and your illegal gambling rings. The young women you've made serve in your whorehouses and the small business owners you squeezed for protection money. And then, if that isn't bad enough, you get yourself into bed with the most unredeemable of your kind imaginable. You crawl between the sheets with terrorists and traitors. You can't live this kind of life and not expect to pay for it sooner or later, Mickey."

"Oh, really?" Gowan said with a measure of false bravado. "And who the hell are you to judge me, huh?"

"I'm not your judge or your jury," the Executioner replied. "I'm your *judgment.*"

And Mack Bolan rid the world of one more contemptible parasite.

Don Pendleton's Mack Bolan

Interception

The city of Split, Croatia, is a multinational den of thieves, where conspiracy, corruption and criminal cells rival for profit and power. Mack Bolan is on its violent streets, trying to stop the global traffickers from doing what they do best—selling death. Fully aware of the mounting odds on all fronts, Bolan is betting on surviving this mission. Again.

*Available May 2009
wherever books are sold.*

JAMES AXLER

DEATH LANDS

Eden's Twilight

Rumors of an untouched predark ville in the mountains of West Virginia lure traders in search of unimaginable wealth. Ryan and his warrior group join in, although it means an uneasy truce with an old enemy. But as their journey reveals more of Deathlands' darkest secrets, it remains to be seen if this place will become their salvation...or their final resting place.

Available June 2009 wherever books are sold.

James Axler
Outlanders®

SHADOW BOX

A new and horrific face of the Annunaki legacy appears in the Arizona desert. A shambling humanoid monster preys on human victims, leaving empty, mindless shells in its wake. Trapped inside this creature, the souls of rogue Igigi seek hosts for their physical rebirth. And no human—perhaps not even the Cerberus rebels—can stop them from reclaiming the planet of their masters for themselves….

Available May 2009 wherever books are sold.